Crossing Over

By

Jennifer Coissiere

Words Mosaic Publications

www.wordsmosaic.com

Covington, GA

Cover Design: Chad Lewis

Cover Layout & Logo Design: Darnetta Frazier

Edited: Shonell Bacon

ISBN: 978-0-9771071-8-6

This book is dedicated to my mother, Angela Hill-Martin. Without you, there'd be no me, and without me, my three beautiful children wouldn't be here. I thank you and love you.

Acknowledgment

Thank you, God, for allowing me to be able to write this story that I know you placed in my heart.

To my wonderful and supportive husband, thank you for standing by me and encouraging me to see this through. I love you.

To my children, Khaila, Xavier, and Elijah, thank you for understanding when I needed to write. I love you all. And I hope you see that anything you put your minds to you can achieve.

I have so many other people to thank. I know I will miss someone, but please blame it on my memory and not my heart.

To my test readers: Sheryl Martin (my sister), Onika Pascal (poet, author, friend), Laryssa

McNeil (friend), and my mother. Thank you all for

your comments. Y'all had my head swollen from the

positive feedback. It's because of you ladies that

I'm working on the sequel.

To Chad Lewis, you created a cover that

exceeded my expectations. Thank you so much for

seeing my vision and bringing it to life.

To author, mentor, and friend, Angelia Vernon

Menchan aka Mama Deep, you rock like pop rocks and

keep it so real. Thank you for helping a newbie out.

To all the wonderful ladies of APOOO Book

Club, the prayers and the wisdom among y'all are so

powerful. Thank you for keeping me lifted and covered

in God's mercy and grace.

To Ava Murray and Darnetta Frazier, both of

you ladies have been there when I needed you. Wishing

you ladies nothing but the best in all you do.

Last, but certainly not least, author, wordsmith, editor extraordinaire, Shonell Bacon, thank you for making sure I had more than just talking heads on the page. Keep it up, Sarge! LOL!

You all have a place in my heart.

To any reader who picks this book up, thanks for giving me a chance. I hope you enjoy reading it as much as I enjoyed writing it. I would love to hear your thoughts. You can email me at wordsmosaic@gmail.com.

Blessings,

Jennifer

Chapter One

The conversation she had with her father Dwight Martin played over and over in her head. Rachelle wanted to make him happy; that's all she really wanted—to make everyone around her happy.

Her father had said to her earlier in the week, "Rachelle, for Christmas all I want from you is for you to be happy. And the gift you can give me and your mother, who is watching you from above," he said pointing up, "is a song. Any song sung from your heart would make me happy."

Rachelle had thought about that day over the past fifteen years, the day she last sang a song from her heart. On that day her heart was broken, and she had never been able to sing that way again. She feared that her singing would take someone else that she loved from her and she wouldn't be able to handle it. But when she had looked into her father's eyes, seeing the worried look on his face, she knew it was time to seek the healing that she needed. Reluctantly, she promised, "I will do it."

He had embraced her, holding her so close in an attempt to let her know it would be alright, and he was proud. Rachelle was shaking inside already. She

didn't know how she would do it, but she would
because she had promised. She had never gone back on
her word before and she wouldn't now. She had to find
a way to overcome all her fears in order to sing from
her heart again.

* * *

Rachelle knew that she would be meeting with the
members of the A.R.T.S. at DeMali's for dinner.
DeMali's was no fancy restaurant; it was a family
owned, down-home, southern style restaurant. They
sold anything you would find in a grandma's kitchen,
including desserts. All the tables were round except
for the booths; the tablecloths were not the usual
gingham—they were white with a vine of mixed flower
embroidery at the bottom. In the center, a large,
opened gardenia was embroidered. Whenever someone
who'd never eaten in DeMali's was seated, they always
asked the same question, "What's with the big flower
in the middle of the table cloth?" The answer was
quite simple, to have more room on the table to put
the food; they added the flowers to the tablecloth
instead of wasting space on a vase. She felt that
DeMali's would be the perfect place to make her
decision official and not back out of her promise to

her father. It was her way of being accountable. She was a firm believer that saying things aloud and to others made things easier to achieve and believe.

Once all the members were gathered around, she didn't waste any time.

"I'm going to sing."

If it wasn't so noisy in the restaurant, the swishing noise of everyone at the table turning their heads at the very same moment would have echoed throughout. All conversation at the table stopped.

She hadn't expected them all to look at her with their eyes bulging out their heads and mouths gaped open. Their reactions were understandable, but unexpected all the same.

Sitting across from her, Raheem, her twin brother, was nodding his head, confirming her statement. Rachelle and he had always been so close; when their father had finished making his request, she had shared with him her promise. He had faith in her that she would be fine. Raheem was beaming with pride.

"You're going to sing what, where, and for who?" asked her best friend Dawn. She was there to witness the loss of Rachelle's voice on that dreaded day so many years ago. She along with Raheem had tried for many years to get Rachelle to sing again like she used to, but their pleas fell on deaf ears.

"I'm going to sing a song," Rachelle replied. "I haven't chosen one yet. In church, for everyone, but mainly for my father."

"I don't believe it. No, I can't believe you're going to sing again," Dawn said. "Can any of you believe it, or am I overreacting?"

"You're overreacting," replied Rachelle. "You don't have to believe it either. I will prove it to you, all of you who doubt me on the day I do sing."

"Come on, Sis," Raheem said, "you know everyone wants to hear you sing. We've been waiting a long time for it. She's overreacting as always, but you are being unreasonable."

"Raheem, everyone hears me on Sunday. Did you forget I sing in the choir, every Sunday?"

"No, but you know what we mean. You're singing solo, that's something totally different. All eyes and ears will be on you," Raheem reminded her.

Kenyon, Raheem's best friend, trying to ease the tension asked, "Why did you decide to bless us with your angelic voice after all these years?" Out of everyone in her close inner circle, Kenyon had been the one person to listen to her without trying to get her to act like what had happened didn't ever occur. He only thought of Rachelle and the pain she was dealing with.

"I'm doing it as a Christmas present for my dad. That's the one thing he's requesting for a present. I couldn't tell him no," Rachelle said, shrugging her shoulders as if it was no big deal, but it was. She and everyone at the table knew singing alone in front of a crowd was difficult for her and had been for quite some time.

"Rachelle, it's really been a long time," Dawn said. "I'll say this and then we'll drop it. Don't let another fifteen years pass by before you sing again. Like Kenyon said, your voice is like that of an angel."

"Thanks, Dawn."

Rachelle turned to the right and embraced Kenyon.

"Thank you," she whispered in his ear. "You've always had my back. I appreciate it."

"Excuse me, can I get any of you anything else?" asked the waitress. No one had noticed her approaching the table.

Wanting to get her full attention, Raheem was the first to respond.

"I believe we're all done here," he said, glancing around at the other occupants of the table. Everyone nodded. "We'll take the check, please?" He really wanted to say with a side order of your name and telephone number, but he wasn't one to set himself up to being turned down in front of his friends and his sister. They'd never let Mr. Smooth himself live it down.

He looked her straight in the eyes. The color of them was mesmerizing to him. He wasn't quite sure why. He only knew he liked looking into her golden honey brown eyes; the attraction was one he'd never experienced before.

"Right away," she answered, popping her gum and turning to walk away.

"DeMali's is starting to fall off," said Dawn. "Did you see her hair and that green bubble gum in her mouth? She has a lack of sophistication and professionalism."

Raheem stared at Dawn. He didn't know where that comment had come from; it was out of character for her. She was usually very quiet, shy, and kept out of the limelight.

"Dawn," Raheem said, "we are at DeMali's not some French bistro. Stop judging her. No one judges you at all, and I can tell you we can find something out of place on you if we really needed to. Do you really think you're any better than she is?"

"Of course I am. How dare you think anything different? Why would you say something like that to me?"

"Why would you say that about her?" he asked, looking at her intensely. He was curious as to what had brought on the sudden ridicule. "You don't even know her, and to be honest, I would never have believed you of all people would ever say such a thing. I've known you most of my life and we don't judge others when we ourselves are not perfect and can be judged, too."

She rolled her eyes at him. *What could he possibly have to judge me on*, she thought.

"You know," Raheem said, "you used to comb your hair in some nice styles, but now all you're wearing is that lazy cap on your head."

Touching her cream-colored crocheted hat, Dawn said, "I do comb my…"

"So why do you wear that thing on your head all the time?" Kenyon asked.

"Kenyon, we live together. You of all people know I comb my hair."

Even though they shared an apartment, Kenyon rarely ever saw her when she wasn't already put together, looking beautiful. "How would I know? I never see you combing anything. See, you really can't judge a person on perception alone."

"It doesn't matter. For the record my hat is a loc cap, not a lazy cap," she said, feeling a bit insulted.

Rachelle intervened as she always did. She was best known for trying to keep the peace.

"Since we are about to go our separate ways until next month, can all the members of A.R.T.S. hold hands and bow your heads. Raheem, please say the closing prayer."

"Heavenly Father, we ask for traveling mercy as we all head toward our next destination. We thank you for this time of fellowship and ask you to keep our days enlightened until we are back in each other's presence. Amen."

"Amen," they all said.

"You all go ahead, I'll pay the bill," said Raheem.

Kenyon turned around, staring at his friend as if it were the first time he'd seen him.

"Mr. Stingy," Dawn said, "you sure you can handle the bill? We don't want you to have a heart attack or anything like that. We know how you get when it comes to your money."

"Let's go before he changes his mind," Rachelle said to Dawn, pushing her toward the door. "My brother doesn't ever offer to pay for anything. Maybe the flip flop in the weather has given him a head cold." The two women chuckled.

Taking a moment, she kissed him on the cheek and said, "Call me when you get home, ok? I love you and thanks."

"Love you, too, little sis."

"Only by two minutes," she said over her shoulder while walking away.

* * *

Raheem was watching the waitress as she walked his way. Her beauty mesmerized him, so much so she seemed to be gliding through the air. When he looked at her beautiful eyes, Raheem could not ignore the all too knowing look he'd seen in his sister's eyes, the dull lifeless look of pain.

"Where did everyone go? They left you to pay their bills?" she asked, handing him the check. Her comment dripped with sarcasm as she thought about the small tip she would certainly receive since everyone else took off.

"I told them to go because I wanted to talk to you alone. I must have missed when you introduced yourself to us. What did you say your name was again?"

"It's Leigh."

"That's a beautiful name for a beautiful person."

"I have a simple name, Leigh Lee. It's as simple as it gets. Are you trying to ask me something other than my name?" She was flirting with him and he knew it. She was hoping maybe she could get him to double the amount of her tip, whatever it would be if she was extra nice to him, pretending she was interested in him.

"Yes, I must admit I am. Was I being that obvious?"

"It was either that or you was going to make a complaint to my manager. No one really cares what our names are until we do something wrong. I hope the service was to your liking, and the food was good. You know the wait staff gets blamed for the food if it sucks even though we didn't prepare it."

"The food was wonderful as always, and you didn't do anything wrong except being so beautiful. Can I have your number and invite you to church?"

"Church?" she said with her face twisted as though she had something bitter in her mouth. "Uh, I don't do nobody's church."

Trying to quickly recover from her dismissal of his offer, Raheem added, "Ok, how about you pick a place? Anyplace you'll feel comfortable in works for me."

"Well I'm off tomorrow. We can go to one of the clubs downtown."

Except that, he thought. Raheem sighed.

He hadn't been to a club since he was in his early twenties. He never understood what the big deal was about clubs. He preferred to go to some place where they could talk, without having to strain their ears or voices. Clubbing wasn't something he liked doing, but it would have to do if he wanted to see her again.

"How about we compromise? Tomorrow I will go to the club with you, but you have to promise me to come to church for our second date, maybe even a meal at my family's house after. My father and twin sister are really great cooks."

"Who said there'd be a second date?" she asked teasingly.

"I'm praying there is one. Remember I did invite you to attend church with me. That should tell you I'm a praying man."

"We'll see."

"I'll let you get back to work. I'll call you tomorrow."

Leigh grabbed his arm before he had the chance to walk away.

"Aren't you forgetting something?"

"Raheem," he said all cocky, impressed that she had even bother to hint at him forgetting to tell her his name.

"No, Raheem," she said, hand extended with her palm facing up. "You forgot to pay me."

Laughing, he looked at the bill. After paying her, he said, "Sorry, I totally forgot. Keep the change and you'll definitely hear from me tomorrow."

"Goodnight, Raheem."

Chapter Two

"Good morning, Rachelle, Dawn. How are you ladies this blessed Sunday morning?"

"Good morning, Pastor Brown. We can't complain," said Dawn as the pastor headed down the hall.

Following his lead, Rachelle said, "I have to get ready for the services."

"See you inside."

"Save me a seat. I need to get to the choir room."

"I will, like I always do," said Dawn.

"I know and I love you for it." Rachelle ran down the hallway. She had to hike up her long matronly dress from around her ankles in an attempt to move faster. She had been waiting to see if she could catch Raheem before the service, but he didn't show up and she had to be on stage in five minutes. It wasn't like Raheem to miss church unless he was sick, and even then he still would show up for praise and worship. The music usually helped him to feel a little better.

Rachelle was saying her prayer for calmness, and the angels to fill her spirit with their heavenly voices as she ran.

Scanning the congregation from the stage, Rachelle's eyes fell on her father, Dawn, Kenyon, but never her brother.

After service, Rachelle met up with the others.

"Hey, Daddy," kissing him on his cheek. "Sorry I didn't wait for you this morning. I was running late as always."

"It's alright, baby," Dwight said, turning his attention to the others. "Dawn, Kenyon, are you guys coming to Sunday dinner today?"

"Of course we are. We've never missed a Sunday dinner in so many years I can't even remember," said Kenyon.

"Let me get on to the house and start on the food. I know how you young people can eat."

"Daddy," Rachelle said, "you act like you're old or something. Nobody can look at you and tell your sixty-five. They'll think you went white prematurely."

"Went white?"

Touching the top of his head, she said, "Yes, Daddy, you went white because this sure isn't gray."

The four laughed.

"They'll know I'm sixty-five if you keep announcing it every chance you get." Holding the door for them as they exit the building, he asked, "Hey Kenyon, where's Raheem?"

"That's a good question, but I can't answer, Mr. D. We haven't seen him today. He never called me Friday night after the A.R.T.S dinner, and I didn't speak to him yesterday either."

"Never mind, I'll see you all later. I know my son will never miss a free home cooked meal."

* * *

"Hey Dad," Raheem yelled, looking all around. He held Leigh's hand, slightly pulling her through the house. "Something sure does smell mighty good up in here."

"We're out on the sun porch. No need to grab a plate, yours is already here on the table waiting for you."

"I still need to grab another one. I brought company with me."

Leigh was nervous. Being around new people intimidated her. She wasn't like them. She hadn't grown up in such a lavish home. Shoot, she wasn't kidding herself; she didn't have anyone to call Dad. "You sure this is ok, and I look fine?" Leigh whispered.

"Yeah, it's fine. You look great in what you have on. This isn't a fancy dinner party. It's just our family's Sunday dinner."

Leigh had slicked back her curly, honey blonde hair, leaving the back in its natural curl. She had on a low cut tight fitting brown shirt with glitter all over the front, accentuating her barely there breast, paired with a stone washed blue denim jean mini-skirt.

All eyes turned toward the doorway, waiting to see who Raheem had brought with him. He never brought anyone around, especially not a female to meet his friends and family. He knew they would be in shock to say the least.

As he entered the sun porch with Leigh on his heels, Raheem watched the only person who really mattered. He watched as Rachelle's eyes grew to the size of the bouncy ball you get from the quarter machines at the grocery store doors. He could tell she was not happy.

"Everyone, this is Leigh," he said. Pointing to the surprised looking faces, Raheem continued on with the introductions. "This handsome gentleman right here is my dad, Dwight Martin. As you can see, I get all my good looks from him." Leigh laughed; no one else found his comment amusing.

"To his right is Kenyon, my best friend. Then there's Dawn, my sister's friend; our Pastor and his lovely wife, Zachary and Zinnia Brown. Zion, what's up man? He's their son. I had no clue he was going to be here. And last but certainly not least, she means the world to me right here, is my twin sister, Rachelle."

"She's your twin? I know you told me you were a twin, but you're not identical," replied Leigh.

Rolling her eyes and shaking her head, Rachelle took a deep breath to calm the feeling of disgust that draped over her. "We are fraternal twins. Which I would say is obvious because identical twins are the same gender, which we clearly are not."

Dwight felt the frost in the air. He jumped up from his usual seat at the head of the table, moving over to sit beside Rachelle to make room for Leigh and Raheem to sit together.

"Well don't keep standing, sit down and eat something," Dwight said to the couple, waving his hand in a downward motion. "Hurry up if you're planning on having dessert. That goes fast here."

Not a sound was made. Everyone was still watching Leigh. She felt as though she was on display in a storefront window.

Turning his attention back to Zion, Raheem stared at him. They'd known each other from the time they were kids dribbling a ball on the basketball courts.

"Zion, how has it been? When did you get back into town?" asked Raheem.

Placing his fork on the side of his plate, Zion wiped his mouth and replied, "I got here last night. I felt like surprising everyone, even Mom and Dad." He chuckled.

"You think you're funny, don't you? You've always liked surprising people, but don't like being surprised yourself," said his mother, Zinnia.

"Mom, it's better to be the one doing the surprising than it is to be the one being surprised."

"Whatever! Leigh, how did you meet, Raheem?"

"I was their waitress."

"Really? Where do you work?" asked Pastor Brown.

Not giving Leigh a chance to respond, Dawn said, "That's why you look familiar to me. I was trying to remember. You're that green bubble gum popping waitress from DeMali's."

"Yeah, that was me," Leigh said proudly.

Clearing her throat as she rose from the table, Rachelle asked, "Does anyone want coffee, dessert, or both?"

"I don't think everyone is quite finished eating their dinner," said Dwight.

"Well I'm done and I wanted to go ahead and get it ready, so no one had to wait. We have homemade sweet potato pie, apple crumb cake, and a peach cobbler with vanilla ice cream of course," she informed the group.

After getting everyone's dessert preference, Rachelle looked at Raheem and asked, "Brother dear, please help me in the kitchen?"

"No, Raheem has company, and they just got here. Let them eat. I'll help you," said Zinnia.

"No, Ms. Zinnia, you're our guest. Raheem will do it." Rachelle and Raheem locked eyes. What her eyes were saying he didn't want to hear. However, seeing the look Rachelle was giving him, Raheem got up. She reminded him of one of his elementary school teachers, with her hair pulled firmly into a bun at the nape of her neck and her lips tightly pursed together. That's all it ever took to spring him into action.

"She's right, Ms. Zinnia. I'll go ahead and help her even though there's only one guest here, and that's Leigh. But I will definitely go anyway," he said trying to sound sweet. But his sweetness would not glaze over the heat radiating from his sister. "Does that make you happy, Rachelle?"

"Yes, it does. Now come on," demanded Rachelle.

As soon as they walked into the kitchen, Raheem asked, "What's your problem, Chelle? Why are you giving Leigh and me the cold shoulder?"

"Why would you pick up trash, bring it home, place it on the dinner table, and serve it cold to your family and friends?"   A look of amazement crept onto Raheem's face.

"Chelle, I can't believe you're acting like Dawn. I guess I'm learning, little by little, I may not really know anyone as well as I thought I did, not even you."

"Don't Chelle me. You know I've always hated being called that ever since…" her voice trailed off. She was now staring in the distance.

Watching, but not saying a word, Raheem realized what really was going on. It had nothing to do with him at all.

"We keep things simple and routine here, Raheem. You know if we are going to do anything different, we inform all the people involved, so there'd be no surprises."

Moving closer to her, Raheem placed his hand on hers.

"I didn't know Pastor and his family was coming over today, no big deal for me."

"I haven't heard from you since I last saw you. Remember I told you to call me. If you didn't call, how would you know? I sure couldn't tell the figment of my imagination and expect you to hear me, now could I?"

"True indeed, you've got a point, but it really isn't that serious. And I'm sorry for being unreachable or around, but you don't have to be like this. Please, all I'm asking from you is for you to give Leigh a chance. There's something intriguing about her. Can you do it for me, please?"

"Fine, but I make no promises. Like she intrigues you, something about her bothers my spirit."

Grabbing the coffee pot and the plates for dessert, Rachelle headed back out to the sun porch. Realizing Raheem was still standing in the same place, she turned and said, "Come on grab the peach cobbler and the ice cream, before you have your guest believing I don't like her, or even worse I dragged you out of here far away from her."

Raheem smiled, doing what he was told.

Chapter Three

"We need to hire someone to answer these phones," said Kenyon. "When we are both with clients, the answering machine works hard. Soft Hands is becoming popular, words getting around."

"I know, but who can we trust in here with our business?"

"I don't know, but we need someone and fast. Do you think your sister would do it a few evenings a week? You know just returning the messages and scheduling the appointments."

Raheem was holding a clipboard in his hand, looking over his upcoming week of appointments. Soft Hands, a massage company Kenyon and he started five years ago, was really doing well. The atmosphere stayed relaxing. Each room had a different type of tranquil oasis about it, which included relaxing sounds as well as the choice of aromatherapy the client desired. The genre décor was that of serenity and peace, the walls were not too bright or dark. It wall were painted a beige, with a vine painted a long the top, right where the ceiling and the wall met.

"We really need someone in the day," said Raheem. "I have an idea about who we can ask."

Kenyon was reluctant to ask, but he needed to know. "Who do you have in mind?"

"Leigh, she can use the extra money."

"No!"

"Just like that, no. Why not?" asked Raheem.

Kenyon took off his glasses, resting them on the receptionist desk. His pupils were dilated, big enough where it almost block out the light brown with flecks of green color of his irises. The tension was building in his neck and jaw line.

"Raheem, use your brains, man, stop thinking with the seat of your pants. You've barely known this girl a month and already you want to trust her with not only your future but also mine. I can't let you do that."

"I know her. I've spent a considerable amount of time with her."

"That's just it. You've spent time with her, but no one else has. She keeps you from your friends and family. I can only imagine what Rachelle is thinking."

"Shut up," Raheem said, pointing his finger at Kenyon. "You know nothing about what Rachelle's thinking."

"You know nothing about what she's feeling or thinking either. You need to calm down and listen. Something you've always had a problem with. Anytime anyone tries to tell you about your family, especially Rachelle, you become Mr. Tough Guy.

"But, see I'm your friend, and I know you, so I'm allowed to speak on them. Leigh has you wrapped up in her world so tight you can't even see something's up with your twin. Don't you have that twin intuition thing?"

"There's nothing wrong with Rachelle. She would've told me," defended Raheem.

"When would she have told you? You don't come to church anymore, you haven't been out with the A.R.T.S. since you met Leigh, and Sunday dinner is a tradition at your father's house. But we haven't seen you since the first time you brought Leigh over, unexpectedly. So, please tell me when would Rachelle have come to speak to you?" Kenyon observed Raheem, but he could not read what he was thinking. "Since she announced that she was going to sing, have you asked her what song? Have you volunteered to help her choose a song? Or simply listen to her practice?"

Raheem couldn't answer because his friend was right. He hadn't been around. He made a mental note to call Rachelle, inviting her to dinner, just the two of them.

"I'm not trying to say it's bad for you to be with Leigh. What I am saying is bring her around, allow the rest of us to get to know her."

"I know you looking out for me. Alright let's call a temp service, get a receptionist for now. Maybe after you spend some time with Leigh, getting to know her a little better, you'll see how awesome she is, and then we can bring her on permanently."

"You've got to learn about not mixing business with pleasure. Although since I'm such a good friend, how about we do a dinner at Dawn's and my apartment? I do need to check with her first, but I can't foresee there being a problem."

"Now that's a great idea. Only the five of us, like old times with a new addition."

"Make it six. I want to hang with Zion before he leaves, again."

"Word, he's leaving again? I thought he was finished with his theological studies."

"Raheem, man you've really been out of the mix of things, for real. No he isn't finished. Just about, but not yet. One more thing, before we go."

"What's that?" he asked curiously.

"I hope you're wrapping it up every time you indulge in the horizontal mambo."

"Man, you aren't right. You know I'm celibate. I must admit I take a lot of cold showers. Believe me it's not because she isn't offering. It's because of my faith and belief in God."

Chapter Four

"You want me to invite Raheem and his low class girlfriend to come over here to break bread with us?" Dawn laughed.

"I'm so tired of you so called Bible toting, believing in God, but still better than everyone else people."

Dawn's eyebrows rose. The Kenyon before her was not the person she knew. He was usually laid back and away from drama. He was the male peacemaker of the group. He tried to make certain no one ever felt out of place. "Don't look at me that way," Kenyon said. "Why don't you want them to come over? Give me one good reason and I'll call Raheem, telling him he can't come."

"I don't have a reason. I was only thinking about how uncomfortable Rachelle would be. You know something is going on with her, that's all. But I honestly haven't given Leigh a chance, and I'm wrong for that."

"You sure that's it? Nothing else I should worry about? Because I heard once when a person has to say honestly, then one is to assume there's more to it than is being said."

Dawn feigned a smile. She felt her face getting hot. "I'm certain, it's nothing else."

"Great then let's do this. It'll be fun, I promise. Plus if it starts getting crazy, we can tell them the party is over and it's time to go."

"Wait! Party? I thought you said dinner, not a party," Dawn said.

"Do you have to always take things so literal? Not a party, it's dinner. Where in our small apartment would we have a party? You need to lighten up."

"Yeah right, lighten up. Let me know what I can do to help, ok," she said as she walked off down the hallway leading to her bedroom.

The apartment wasn't that large, but the setup was ideal for them to have their own space and privacy. The kitchen and living room served as a divider, separating their bedrooms and bathrooms on either end of the apartment.

Inside Dawn's room, she had a twin size bed, allowing for more space to create her hair clips and her jewelry. Another part of her life she kept a secret from the others. She'd been selling them in the boutique for about a year; clients were coming in requesting custom pieces as gifts for friends.

It was in the privacy of those four walls, behind her locked door, she would take off her loc cap, allowing her locs to hang free. No one had seen her hair in ages.

She went over to her closet and took down a box of keepsakes she had saved over the years. A few birthday cards from her parents, the last picture she took with her parents before they left, a picture of her aunt Rebecca, and sketches she did in her teen years. The last item she pulled out from the box was a picture of Raheem, Rachelle, and her. She stood between them with the biggest grin on her face. These few items signified the happiness and the sadness in her life.

Dawn was raised by her aunt Rebecca, the only family she had in Georgia. Her parents had become missionaries, and Rebecca had taken her in, believing she didn't need to be trekking through the backwoods of the Philippines. Keeping her stable and in touch with where she came from.

She would pull out her grandmother's small cedar box that had kept many important papers, when her mother and aunt were children. Now it held the letters and pictures her mother wrote to her once a month. Some were open, others still sealed with the thoughts and chronicles of what her parent were up to, unknown to her. She prayed for the day where she would open a letter and her mother would have written a date of return to the states.

Her favorite picture of her mother was in the cedar box. It was the day she had brought her home from the hospital all bundled up, held close to her heaving bosom. She could see the love and joy radiating off her mother, even in that old picture. It was only five short years later, when her parents said God had put it their hearts to go where they were needed more. The people in the Philippines really needed them to help with their missions work. Off they went to build schools, hospitals, and churches; while Dawn stayed behind and longed for their return.

She was lonely due to her aunt never getting married or having children of her own. When she saw Rachelle and Raheem, she wanted to be their friend because of how close they were. She never had that with anyone, especially not since she was an only child.

She was drawn to the gentle way Raheem cared for Rachelle as if she was a fragile piece of painted glass. But he never treated Dawn the same way. He respected her, was kind to her, but it wasn't exactly what she was looking for. Sometimes figuring out what she wanted confused her more than it made sense.

Chapter Five

"Are you finally ready to get to know the other important parts to my life? Do you want to get to know my sister and my friends a little better?"

"I'm not trying to be mean," Leigh said, "but what do I need to know them for? It's not like they like me or anything. You're all I need. I don't need them."

"But I do. I want you to be a part of my life as well as theirs. It means a lot to me."

"Maybe we should quit seeing each other then," Leigh said, shaking her leg.

"Don't you like having people around? You've been hanging with me so much when do you find time to see your other friends? I know I don't have the extra time between you and work."

Uncrossing her legs, Leigh stood and walked behind the sofa. Her hands found Raheem's shoulders and began massaging him. She kissed his neck. He jumped.

"Hold on, I told you already. I have too much respect for you to cross that line right now." He'd grabbed her hands, stopping her from putting her hands down his shirt.

"Don't you find me pretty?"

"Yes, I do, but that's beside the point. I don't want to do this."

"Do what? All I'm doing is helping you to relax," she said, rubbing her hands down his chest.

He grabbed her hands again. This time ducking under her arms, he spun around to face her with his knees in the couch, feeling the urge to kiss her pouty lips. Instead he bit down on the inside of his cheek.

"Why do you do that? Every time I ask you about your friends or your family, you throw yourself at me."

Leigh's hands flew to her hips. "You think I throw myself at you? Do you know how many men would love to be in your place?"

"I don't care about anybody else being with you. I'm trying to get to know you better. I have no hidden agenda, but if you need it to be physical, then I'm not the one for you."

"What do you want from me, Raheem?" she asked exasperated.

"I want to get to know you before I get to know that part of you." He tilted his head in the direction of her lower body.

"Fine. I will tell you. I hope you can deal with it."

Raheem took a seat, giving her his undivided attention. Clasping his hands on his lap, he waited.

Leigh paced the floor. This is what they all asked for, to know about her past, but once they found out, they disappeared. Nobody ever wanted to love the girl who never experienced love and if she did doesn't know it.

"Do you know how it feels to be given away, to never belong to anyone, not even yourself?" she asked.

He shook his head no, but didn't utter a word. He didn't want her to stop talking due to anything he may have said. He made a mental note to try to be like his sister, keeping his face in a neutral position. Not giving any indication of how her rhetorical questions were affecting him.

"Imagine growing up in a group home. There were only girls, no boys at all, not even the counselors or anything like that." She chuckled, swinging her arms back and forth. "Those other girls said their parents were going to come back for them, you know, they were going through some things and needed to heal or find themselves. Not me, I had no way of knowing. I never heard from anyone. Who am I kidding, I knew no one."

He took a chance asking her, "Didn't you ever go to a foster home?"

"Oh sure I did. As I got older and my body started changing, no one wanted to keep me around. They said I was too pretty to be around their husbands and their teenage sons. To keep me around would be a risk to their family's freedom. These were people who attended church on a regular basis, too.

"They wanted me to believe in their God even though they didn't have enough faith in him to believe he would keep them from deterring from what they knew was right. Besides, why should I believe in a man I can't see?"

Only thing that came to his mind were the lessons he learned in Bible school when he was growing up. He remembered being told to say thank you for Mommy, Daddy, my sister, and for waking me up this morning. He tried using that technique but gearing it toward Leigh's situation. "He gave you life, that's why you should believe. Don't let anyone stop you from believing. Thank him for keeping you safe and putting breath in your lungs every day."

"I can't stop, I've never believed. I've never had a reason to believe. Let me ask you this one important question. Why would the man of all creations bring me to life, allowing my parents to give me away?"

She couldn't even remember what it was like to be within the arms of any relatives. The only reason she knew that her mother hadn't died is because when she was in the foster homes, they always brought her to the agency once a month on the third Friday of the month, anticipating that her mother would show up for her visit. She never did. After a while she stopped hoping and looking forward to the day. No one ever told her maybe if she prayed a tad bit harder someone, anyone related to her by blood would show up. Maybe even saying to her it's time for you to come home where you belong. Nope there was no reason to believe in heaven or a God. He simply couldn't be real and allow her to be alone, even now.

"We can't dwell on the things we cannot change, such as your parents," Raheem said. "Whoever they were they knew it was not in their power to take care of you, and you'd be better off where you were."

"You say that because you have family, but it's still not the answer to my question."

It was a-ha moment Raheem would never forget. He realized more than ever that he had to bring his sister and Leigh together; they had more in common than he first realized. Together, he believed they could heal each other's heart from the sense of loss.

Rationalizing hadn't worked in convincing Leigh to fellowship with his friends; the only option he had left was to beg.

"What will it take for you to have dinner with the people I care about? I know I might regret saying this, but I'll do just about anything."

He held his breath, waiting for her payment for one night of things unknown.

She licked her lips in a seductive way, making him certain the sinister look upon her face could only mean she wanted one thing and one thing alone. He braced himself for what was to come, wondering would he be able to do it.

"Have a few drinks with me," she said.

Raheem did a double take. *Did I hear her correctly*, he thought.

"A few drinks, that's all it will take?" he asked confused.

"Of course, you can show me you're not a complete bore after all."

A sigh of relief escaped his lips.

"From the look on your face, you thought…" she couldn't finish her statement. She was laughing too hard.

* * *

While swallowing one drink after the next with Leigh, Raheem had found himself relaxing more and more. She told him contrary to what people thought of her, she did graduate from high school. She had wanted to attend college, but didn't have the money to go, plus she had no clue what she wanted to do with her life besides partying. After awhile, things got fuzzy, and Raheem was having difficulty remembering what was real and what was a part of his dreams. No matter how hard he fought, his eyelids got heavier, making it impossible to keep his eyes open.

Raheem lay with his eyes closed for a moment once he awakened. When he rolled over, he was disoriented. Opening his eyes, Raheem stared at the ceiling; he wasn't quite sure where he was. He was trying to figure out how long he had been asleep. His tongue felt thick in his mouth, and the pounding in his head made him feel extremely nauseated. Stretching his arms out, he slowly turned his head to the left when his hand landed on what felt like someone's body. His mind was screaming no, as he saw the last person he wanted to see laying in his bed. Dawn.

Chapter Six

"Daddy, have you seen Raheem lately?"

"In order to have seen him, I would've needed to speak to him first, and I've done neither. But let's not worry about him. I want to talk about you. I've allowed you to wander around lost for far too long."

Rachelle looked surprised. She never liked when anyone turned their attention solely on her. That's part of the reason behind her never letting anyone get too close to her. When they became more than associates or friends in passing, they believed they held a position which warranted unwanted questions.

"Rachelle, are you listening to me?" Dwight asked her. Concern showed on his face, partly due to him calling her name for a few minutes, and the lack of response from her.

She flinched once he touched her shoulder, focusing her eyes to actually see him standing in front of her. "I'm sorry, Daddy. I drifted off for a second. What did you say?"

"I asked what you would be singing for the holiday program at church."

"The choir-"

"No, not the choir," he cut her off. "I asked about you. Remember you promised to grace me with a song as a gift. I know you have plenty of time to think about it because it is after all only October, but this time of year goes by quick."

"Yes, Daddy, I remember. I don't know yet. Could I convince you to let me buy you a present instead? Maybe I can send you on a trip for a week?"

Dwight sighed. "Can I ask you a question, Rachelle?"

"Of course you can, Daddy. You can ask me anything you want, anytime you want."

"Alright, tell me why you don't want to sing anymore. Then tell me what I can do to make you want to sing like you used to."

"Give her back to me, then I will enjoy it again," she answered with that distant look in her eyes.

"I can't bring her back, Rachelle. You're not the only one who misses her." Grabbing her by the shoulder, Dwight turned her to face him. "You must know by now if I could bring her back, I would've. Baby, I miss her more than you can ever imagine. She was my breath, my heart, my night and my day, my life and my soul mate."

Resting her head on his chest, she asked, "If you miss her, Daddy, how do you go on with your life?"

"I have to, don't you know why?"

Rachelle shook her head vigorously, tears beginning to pool in the corner of her eyes.

"I have to keep living for you and Raheem. If I gave up on life what would become of the two of you, especially you?" Her heart broke for her father; that was the push the tears in her eyes needed to spill over on to her cheeks.

"You had her longer than I did. Raheem had you, but I had nobody. My mommy, my best friend was taken from me, before I was ready to be on my own," she cried. "She was supposed to teach me how to be a respectable woman, a wife, and a mother. Now I don't know if I can ever love the way I ought to."

"You've had us, Pastor Brown, Ms. Zinnia, Raheem, Kenyon, Zion, and Dawn. We've all been there for you." He sighed. "And, baby, love is not taught. It's something you just know how to do when it's time to do it. Once you have love in your heart for someone, everything else comes naturally."

"It's not the same. I wanted my mother, the woman who sang me to sleep when I was little. Did you know she used to come into my room when she thought I was asleep and stare at me?" A small smile appeared on her lips.

Dwight smiled. "No, I didn't know that." He remembered when she would tell him she would be right back. Sometimes she would be gone for so long that when she returned to the room, he would be fast asleep. Lily was always checking to make sure they weren't too hot or too cold, double checking that the doors were locked properly, making sure they were all safe from harm.

Maybe that's where they had gone wrong with Rachelle. She probably smothered her too much with her love and her protection.

"I would lie as still as I could. Never wanting her to leave and I knew if she realized I was awake, she would leave because she didn't want to keep me from getting my rest. I listened to her breathe. She took long, deep breaths. After awhile it would lull me to sleep. Once she died, no one came. It was the hardest time for me to ever sleep."

"Is that why you'd crawl into Raheem's bed?"

She nodded. "Yes."

"Why didn't you come to me? I am your father." A pang of jealousy laced with hurt gagged Dwight.

"I know, but I needed a connection to her. I'm not trying to hurt you, Daddy, but Raheem had her blood coursing through his body. When I'm near him it's as if I can feel her touching my spirit."

"I understand. That doesn't stop me from being concerned with how long you've been grieving. It's been fifteen years. You need to move on with your life. If I know Lily, she'd want you to find happiness again." She'd want that for all of them he thought.

"That's easy for you to say. You had her with you longer than we did. I'm not ready to let her go yet."

"Rachelle, I don't want you to forget her. I want you to become a part of society again."

She looked frightened.

"I can't."

Confused, Dwight asked, "You can't or you won't?"

"I can't or I will hurt again." Whenever she thought she could do it, her dreams were plagued with friends and family talking to her one-minute and the next they disappeared right in front of her.

"I think you need to seek some help. I should've made you go as soon as Lily died. If I had done right by you, then you'd be a different person today."

"I won't go. I have you and Raheem."

"Honey, Raheem is trying to have a life of his own. You need to do the same. And I'm not getting younger. I'm going to join your mother one day."

"Stop it!" she yelled. "Stop it! No one is going anywhere. Not you, not Raheem."

Raheem walked in as she was screaming. He grabbed Rachelle pulling her into his protective arms.

"Tell him, Raheem, please," she cried into his chest.

"Tell him what?"

"You're not leaving me and neither is he."

"While you're at it, tell her she needs to get help dealing with her emotions," their father said.

Raheem held Rachelle close. "Calm down," he said as he rubbed her back. "Right now we're all healthy, so you have nothing to worry about." He exchanged an all too familiar look with his father.

Dwight shook his head, held up one finger, but never said whatever it was that he was thinking. He'd let it go for now.

"We'll talk about what you and Dad were talking about later. Alright?"

He looked into his sister's eyes. She looked so lost and afraid, but she nodded nonetheless.

"I came over here on a mission," Raheem said.

Rachelle raised an eyebrow. "What kind of mission?"

"To ask you two things. First, I want to invite you to dinner, just you and me."

"Ok, what's the other thing?" she asked never bothering to acknowledge his first request.

"The second is another dinner invitation, but this one would consist of a few friends. Over at Kenyon and Dawn's apartment."

"I can do that." She nodded. "We can do that."

Raheem smiled. "Ok, well where do you want to eat?"

* * *

Rachelle and Raheem decided to go back to his apartment, where they would cook together.

"I'm sorry for ignoring you these last few weeks."

"Are you really?" she asked while popping a jalapeno into her mouth along with a guacamole-covered chip.

"We've been busy at work. We need to find someone to cover the receptionist spot. Also, I really like Leigh. Something about her has my attention and I'm not sure what it is."

"I don't know her, so I can't say what it is."

"Chelle, you may never know what it is. You're my sister, and you can't know things like what attracts me to a woman. Sometimes you have to be happy for me and nothing else."

"I will be happy when I have a reason to be happy. Raheem, why do you like calling me a name I have asked you not to call me?" She rested her chin on her steepled fingers.

"I called you Chelle all the time when we were little. Ever since Mommy died, you won't allow anyone to call you anything but your full name. I like having a nickname for you."

"Can't you see that's the reason why I don't like it? Mommy gave me my nickname. She always called me Chelle. The only time she called me Rachelle was when I was in trouble." She reached over to hold Raheem's hands. "I feel like I'm in trouble, right now, and I don't know when I'll ever feel any differently. How do you do it, Raheem?"

"How do I do what?"

"How do you still go on, like nothing drastic ever happened in our life?"

"I take one day at a time. I pray really hard for God to give me strength, the kind of strength I will need to be there for you and Dad if I need to be there. All of us can't walk around lost. And I'm the boy and the oldest."

"You always talking about being the oldest like we are years apart," she said, smiling. She loved having her big brother, but equally loved teasing him about the two-minute difference.

"I like to see you smile and I know making that comment does it every time. I want to see you heal, smile, and have a family of your own one day. Which brings me to Dad's request. Rachelle, you need to seek help."

She opened her mouth to speak, but he patted her hand, and added, "Rachelle, I think you should consider what Dad's telling you." He raised his hand to stop her from protesting. "Give me a chance to explain. I'm not saying to go to a lab coat wearing, lay on the couch and tell me what you see when you look at the white boards with the black dots creating vague images. How about going to counsel with Pastor Brown or Ms. Zinnia? It won't be the same as speaking to a stranger, and they knew Mommy, so they would be more in tune with what you are going through."

She shook her head.

Raheem sighed. "Did you at least pick a song to sing for Dad?"

Her eyes brightened for a moment. "I thought maybe I would sing "I'll Be Home for Christmas" or maybe "Silver Bells." I guess I'm not sure. I'm still really nervous and feel like my back is up against the wall."

"Why do you feel that way?"

She tugged on the collar of her high neck brown dress. "What if I can't sing as good as I used to? What if someone else…" Her voice got lower as she wished the last part of her question. It was so low that Raheem didn't hear her; however, he knew what she was asking already.

"Rachelle, I'm begging you to please get some help. Surely, you don't believe that someone is going to die because you sing. God gave you a wonderful gift. Don't take it for granted."

"I'll think about it."

Slamming his hands down on the table, scaring her and himself, he spoke in a firm voice. "You need to do this and there is nothing for you to think about. Do you understand you could help others get past their pain if you would get over yours? It's been fifteen long years. No one should suffer this long. Mommy must be rolling over in her grave knowing you've given up on life. That's it, you gave up on life."

"Please stop yelling at me," she whispered. "If it will make you happy, I will do it. But please stop the…" Tears choked her. He'd never spoken to her in such a way before.

"It will make me happy, but you should do it to make you happy. I should not matter. It's time for you to cross over into the realm of the living."

Chapter Seven

"Abiding Faith Tabernacle, this is Rachelle. How may I help you today?"

Flipping through the pages of the desk calendar, Rachelle looked for the next available date to do a baby's dedication.

"Mrs. Fletcher, we can do it on Sunday, October 22. You do remember all dedications are done at the second service? Ok if anything changes you know the number to call. Have a blessed day."

"Hello, Rachelle. How are you doing?"

Turning around, she found Zion leaning against her desk looking as handsome as ever.

"I'm doing fine and you?

"I can't complain because someone else is bound to be struggling more than I am."

"You want to talk about it?" she asked. "I'm a good listener."

"There's nothing to talk about, but if you'd like to catch up on old times, I'd love that more than anything else."

"Really now, are you sure about that? Are you feeling nostalgic, or is it because you're returning to school soon and you will miss us?"

"I guess you can say a little of both."

"Then I would be honored, but of course I have to finish up the work day. You do know I'm on the clock, right?"

"I know, but you can be daring, live a little, spontaneous and adventurous. Tell my dad you're feeling ill and want to go home to lie down," he coaxed her.

"I thought you were going to school to become a pastor like your dad. Pastors don't tell lies."

"If you're afraid to disappoint them," Zion said, smirking, "I'll do it. If they ever find out, which I doubt, you can always say it was all my idea. And that will be the truth."

"I can't allow you to do that. It wouldn't be right."

"You're so untouched."

"Huh?" she said, not understanding exactly what he meant.

"You're pure in every sense of the word. I've never met anyone like you."

"Is that a bad thing?"

"No."

"Then why did you say it like I had the plague or something?"

"I didn't mean anything, it was a compliment. Can't you see when you've been giving one and accept it without asking any questions?"

She stared at him, not certain if she wanted to answer. She would have to admit to herself and Zion her naiveté, her inexperience of being in a conscious world.

It was at that moment she began her to understand her family's request. Even though she had agreed to seek help, she'd only agreed for the sake of her loved ones. Now, she knew it wasn't going to be enough to do it for them. In order to successfully overcome the obstacles in her way, she would have to commit to healing for herself and no one else.

Zion was watching her quietly, observing her eyes darting from side to side.

"You can teach me," she said. "Only if you'd like to, I don't want you to feel burdened with showing me things I should have known by now. After all I'm grown, and I need to act as such."

Zion walked to her, but didn't touch her; it wouldn't be right for him to place his hands on a woman who hadn't invited him to do so. The air between the two was dense, a tension neither noticed before.

A not so innocent look danced in his eyes, and with voice having dropped an octave or two lower, he said, "I'd love to show you the ways of the world, all the ways."

Chapter Eight

Dawn looked around, making sure everything was in its place, fluffing the pillows on the couch one more time. "They'll be here any minute," she announced. "We promised Raheem we'd give Leigh a better chance than we did before, so let's do our best." She would try to fake it as much as she could, but the truth of the matter was, she didn't want to get to know Leigh any better. Having Leigh in her space was overwhelming.

Dawn had watched how Raheem follow her as she went from table to table doing her job that night at DeMali's. His eyes didn't leave her presence much while they were eating and fellowshipping with each other. Even though Dawn hadn't worked that hard to get him to notice her, with Leigh now taking all his time and attention Raheem would never realize the passion she had growing inside her for him. The desire was at times over bearing and she hadn't a clue why. He'd never shown her any signs of being interested in her other than being a friend to her through association with Rachelle.

The only other time they came close to having anything, Raheem didn't seem to remember. However,

Dawn still recalled the way she felt when she awoke beside Raheem. She would never forget the night they had shared. She only hoped Raheem would one day recall the connection they had.

A set of quick loud knocks on the door signaled they had arrived. Each person put on a welcoming smile.

Kenyon said, "If no one else is going to open it, I will," walking over to the door.

"Hey, y'all come on in. I hope you're hungry," Kenyon said to the couple. Turning back to everyone already in the apartment, he said, "You remember Leigh right?"

Rachelle was the first to acknowledge Leigh. Draping an arm around both Leigh's and Raheem's shoulder, she led them into the apartment.

"Leigh, welcome to our little get together. Make yourself at home. I want to apologize for not giving you a fair chance before." Rachelle, being her typical self, held a welcoming smile that only she could pull off. Whatever she was thinking, no one could tell because she had kept her face neutral from all emotions except for that dutiful smile.

She looked at Raheem; he didn't say a word. He let Leigh decide for herself what to believe. Maybe she would be able to let her guard down and make new friends.

"No sweat. I understand."

"Let's not dwell anymore than needs be on the past. Let's eat, I'm starved," Dawn said.

She and Raheem locked eyes for a quick moment, but they broke it almost immediately.

"Something smells wonderful," said Leigh.

"Kenyon will have to take all the credit for this. Usually when we all get together like this, we all chip in and cook or bake something, but not tonight."

If his pride would let him, he would have been blushing, but he just waved his hand at Dawn trying to get her to be quiet.

Rachelle whispered in Dawn's ears, "Stop embarrassing him in front of company."

"Girl, please this is what he lives for, attention from a woman."

"So Leigh, do you have any family here in Georgia?" asked Zion.

"I don't have any family, anywhere."

Eyes bore into her from all sides; everyone had family somewhere. Raheem came to her rescue.

"She doesn't know any of her family. She grew up in a group home."

"Oh ok. Well what do you do for fun?" Rachelle asked.

"I uh, um…go to the clubs and drink," she said nonchalantly.

The response she got was not surprising. It was pure silence. Raheem placed a reassuring hand on the center of her back. Turning she smiled at him. The tension he felt drained from his body, slowly. There was a possibility they all could be friends.

The acceptance of Leigh into their friendship circle was not the only thing grating on his nerves. He was still trying to figure out how did he gone from hanging out, drinking with Leigh to ending up in bed with Dawn.

The morning she woke up neither said a word. She got dress and left the hotel room. All he knew was they were both naked and nothing else.

"Ok let's try something different to stay positive and not dampen a potentially wonderful evening. Maybe you should ask us questions instead," Rachelle suggested.

"Alright, Kenyon the first question is for you. What did you cook?"

Laughter erupted.

"Amarillo arroz con pollo, y épinards à la crème."

"Are you Spanish?"

Dawn playfully slapped him in the back of his head.

"What's that for?" he asked as innocent as he could.

"You know we don't know what that is. And no he isn't anything close to a Latino."

"How you know I'm not a little Latino? You know everyone is always claiming to be one-quarter Cherokee Indian. I went a different route. Any way we are having yellow rice and chicken with creamed spinach."

"Man, you need to let that go. You going to have Leigh thinking we are all crazy, but that's an honor you can have all alone," Zion said.

"Leigh, you get to sit at the head of the table across from Zion. Everyone else pick your seat,

they're our guests, so they get to sit at the heads
of the table, to be made to feel honored," said
Kenyon.

"Thanks, I could have sat at one of the other
seats," said Leigh. "I don't mind really."

"It's our way. We do it this way. Anytime
anyone comes over especially for the first time, we
make sure they feel welcomed and special by the time
they leave."

"Consider it a good deed," said Dawn.

"Before we take our seats, if we can join
hands, and bless the food," Rachelle said. "Dawn
since you're the hostess, if you don't mind could you
do the honor, please?"

Reluctantly, Leigh placed her hands in Dawn's
and Raheem's. Raheem squeezed her hand, trying to
calm the anxiety she was obviously feeling.

"Almighty father, I say thank you for this day,
for the chef, and a time to fellowship with old
friends and new friends. I ask for you to allow the
food we are about to take part of, to do as they
should, in nourishing our bodies, our minds and our
spirit, in the name of your son, Jesus Christ, amen.
Now let's eat."

"Amen," said the others, everyone except Leigh.

"How long have you all known each other?" Leigh asked.

"We all met at different times, but for the most part we grew up together," said Zion.

"So were you all born in Georgia or did you migrate here later on?"

Pointing to his sister and back to himself, Raheem answered, "We were born and grown right here."

"Yes, I'm a real Southern Belle," Rachelle said. Everyone else laughed except for Zion. In his eyes she really was a southern bell.

"I'll go next," said Dawn. "I'm not from here. I was born in Salisbury, North Carolina. I moved her to live with my aunt Rebecca."

"Did something happen to your parents?"

"No, heavens no," she answered startled at the thought. Whenever she prayed, it was always for the safe return of her parents. "My parents are missionaries, and my aunt didn't think it was wise for me to be growing up in a foreign country. So I ended up here. No we didn't attend the same school, but we did and still do worship at the same church."

"Wow, have you gone to visit them? Have they been back?" Leigh asked very curious to know more.

"You know they come back every couple of years, mainly for important occasions. It's been a while because I didn't go to college, so I didn't have another graduation for them to come to. I guess their next big visit it will be when I get married. Now a secret that many don't know, I am afraid to fly, so no I haven't gone to see them in the Philippines as yet. "

"Kenyon, you can go before me," said Zion.

"Alright, I grew up with the twins. Our parents are related."

Shock appeared on Dawn's face. She'd known them for many years and they never disclosed that bit of information.

Kenyon continued. "It's always been so simple to tell people we're best friends because even though we're really cousins, I've felt more like their brother. I was born here as well."

Finally coming out of her shock, Dawn asked the question bubbling within her, "Did you guys forget to tell me this little bit of information? If Mr. Dwight is your uncle, why do you call him Mr. D instead of Uncle D?"

"I don't know. What does it matter, I'm still respectful when I speak to him. By now you should be calling him Uncle D you've been around long enough."

"We'll talk about it later, OK," Rachelle reassured.

"Last but not least, Zion, spill it. Can you top these guys?" asked Raheem.

"I'm a preacher's son. We didn't move around a lot as far as our home goes, but it took sometime before my father finally found the location where we're at now. It had to be right, or else he would not settle for it. I'm from Georgia as well, but a city two hours from here."

"Well you are an eclectic bunch. I have one other silly question, and it's for you, Dawn." Everyone turned to look at Leigh while she in turn focused her attention on Dawn.

"Well go ahead. I have nothing to hide. What do you want to know?"

"Your um, thing that's on your head is beautiful. I remember at the restaurant seeing you with one on and admiring it at that time as well. Any way my question for you is do you always have your hair covered and what are you hiding underneath it?"

Dawn had been wearing those loc caps for so long, everyone was interested in her answer. She had their undivided attention. She on the other hand was contemplating how she wanted to answer the question. It was moments before she said she had nothing to hide, but Leigh proved her wrong. There she was eating her words, and truly not understanding why. What was there for her to hide; they'd either love it or hate it, but they would have to accept it.

She was hiding the person she'd become from them and it was time to let them in on the rest of her that they were unaware of. Rather than answering with words, Dawn slowly pulled off her loc cap, revealing what she's been hiding for some time. When the cap came off, completely, hanging from her head was the most beautiful, well groomed locs touching her shoulders.

"Dawn, you look gorgeous. Why have you hidden this from us all this time?" asked Rachelle.

Shrugging her shoulders, she said, "I guess we all have secrets we need to reveal. For us to be so

close there's so much we don't know about each
other."

"That doesn't matter to me right now. I want to
know can I touch your hair." Rachelle began reaching
out, but waited for Dawn's approval.

Leaning her head in Rachelle's direction, Dawn
said, "Go ahead."

"Leigh, we were supposed to get to know you
better, but we learned a lot more about each other.
We have to do this again," said Kenyon.

Raheem and Leigh smiled. They were beginning to
accept her.

* * *

"I had a good time tonight. What did you think
of Leigh?" asked Kenyon.

Rachelle couldn't deny it; she wasn't half bad
at all. Her haste to keep her brother to herself
blinded her in an almost jealous rage. "She's sweet,
young, but sweet. And Raheem seems smitten by her, so
I'm happy."

Using her delight, Zion saw an opportunity to
reveal feelings he's been keeping to himself for
years. Rachelle was such a gentle flower; he wasn't
sure how to approach her without frightening her.

"I'm going to miss hanging with you." Quick to cover his remarks, he added, "I mean everyone until I get back from school."

Reassuring him she said, "You don't have much time left there. It will go by really quick."

After the dinner, Zion and Rachelle had a taste for something sweet. They decided on the always popular desire for ice cream. Driving over to the Brewster's, they walked up to the shop and peered into the window. It was hard to believe in the tiny building they made ice cream and ice cream cakes and had freezers large enough to keep all the ice cream cold and still had room to serve the ice cream lovers.

They had some of the best ice cream either had tasted in a long while. They sat on one of the few benches sparsely placed around the building.

Rachelle broke the silence.

"Do you plan on preaching at Abiding Faith?"

"I believe that's what's expected of me." His answer was puzzling to her. It wasn't what she'd expected.

"I'm sorry did I miss something? You didn't answer my question. Are you going to preach there because you want to or because it's what is expected from you?"

She'd hit a nerve. Rachelle saw his muscles twitch in his face, brows furrowing. Suddenly his dessert was no longer tasty. He threw it away, using the small moment of time to think of the proper answer.

"I won't tell a soul what you say," Rachelle said. "Remember I'm a good listener, a good friend, and not a gossip warrior."

She was relentless when she wanted to be. Knowing she would continue to press him for an answer to a question he tried not to focus on, he turned to look at her, deciding it was better said to someone he could trust than to continue to avoid his feelings.

"I guess I can tell you." He hesitated a moment. The quickening of his pulse signaling to him he was more afraid of his true feelings than he had realized, but he went on anyway. "I wonder from time to time, if I'm doing the right thing becoming a preacher. I feel I'm doing this for the wrong reason."

"I'm not at a place where I can tell you if you're doing the right thing or not, but I can tell you one thing."

Paying close attention to what she was about to say next, Zion stopped twirling the paper napkin into a skinny spiral, hanging on her every word. "Go ahead I'm listening."

"Don't lose sight of yourself in place of someone else."

"Let me ask you, how do you or better yet, where do you get your inspirations, ideas on the things you do?"

Looking at him in a way that told him he should've already known without having to ask, Rachelle point to the sky and mouthed the word "Pray."

He thought, *I've been praying, now I need to listen.*

Chapter Nine

In taking the first steps toward letting her mother go, Rachelle scheduled an appointment with Pastor Brown and requested Ms. Zinnia to be there as well.

Having her office next door to the Pastor's, she'd arrived a little early, using the time to really take in the vastness of the office.

Pastor Brown's office was decorated simple, but chic. The solid mahogany desk was placed across from the door; two straight, leather backed and cushioned chairs sat in front of the desk, which housed on the other side a leather swivel chair. A mahogany corner bookcase stood in the left corner of the office, displaying on the shelves besides the variation of Bibles, a picture of Pastor Brown, Ms. Zinnia and Zion.

Rachelle was holding the picture, staring at what she thought to be an ideal picture perfect family captured on glossy paper forever. Ms. Zinnia walked in soundlessly and approached Rachelle. When she touched the wooden frame, Rachelle jumped. "Ms. Zinnia, I was just-"

"Hush, child. Don't act as if you got caught with your hand in my purse," Ms. Zinnia joked. She recognized the ever pining look, on Rachelle's face, to have what she couldn't get back; a complete family consisting of mother, father and brother.

"How are you, Ms. Zinnia?"

"I am blessed and highly favored." Zinnia took the picture, rubbing her right hand over the glass. She smiled as she recalled the memories of that picture. "You know this picture was taken the day Zion told us his decision to become a pastor. We were so excited. He'd finally found his calling."

If they can't see through the façade Zion's wallowing through, Rachelle thought, *then how would they be able to help me?*

Pastor Brown walked in and gave both ladies a quick embrace before sitting behind his desk and pulling out a legal size yellow writing tablet. Rachelle and Ms. Zinnia took the seats facing him.

"Alright, Rachelle," Pastor Brown began, "what did you want to see us for? Normally, as you already know, either Zinnia does the counseling or I do it. The only time we counsel together is when it's a couple's session. But we've known you for such a long time we decided to honor your request."

"Thank you both for being here. I know your time is precious and you're very busy servicing the members of the church. But I feel I needed you both. Pastor Brown," she said looking him in the eyes, "I needed your expertise of what God would want me to do." Turning to face Ms. Zinnia, she added, "Ms. Zinnia, I need you to be the mother figure I've been missing for the past fifteen years."

"We've been waiting for you to come to us all these years," said Zinnia, touching her shoulder lightly.

"We told your father that our doors were always open day or night. But the only person ever to come was Raheem."

Exchanging glances of confusion, Pastor Brown and Zinnia noticed they were not alone in their perplexity. Rachelle's facial expression was blank.

"You did know Raheem had come to talk to us right?" asked Pastor.

Slapping her hands on her thighs, Rachelle said, "How would I know if everyone was and is always keeping some kind of secret from me? No one ever wanted to tell me anything. Too afraid I was going to break or something."

"Don't get upset. You have to think back over the course of the years, evaluate the condition, the state of mind you were in emotionally and spiritually," said Pastor Brown.

"I was living," Rachelle said through gritted teeth. "Why is it so hard for everyone to understand I was still living and my mother she was dead?"

"We understand you were hurting, but what did you do to get past the pain?"

Rachelle looked at Ms. Zinnia thinking of how she'd been taking care of her brother and father. Washing their clothes, cooking their meals, and making sure the house was clean, warm and inviting.

"She didn't ask to die, but I prayed to God almost every day to take me so I could be with my mother." Rachelle got up, walking over to the window behind Pastor Brown's desk. Staring at nothing in particular she said, "But he never answered my prayers and I stopped asking him. I still believed in him. One day it all made sense to me. God wanted me to stay around to be there to take care of my father and my brother in the place of my mother. I did what needed to be done."

"No, baby, you shut down and tuned out the world," Pastor Brown said. "If it didn't go on inside of your four bedrooms, three and a half bathroom, single family dwelling, it never happened. That's hiding from life.

"Your actions when Raheem brought that nice young lady over should tell you something was wrong. You know she entered into your tranquil haven, without your permission and that meant you were no longer in control."

Zinnia gave Pastor Brown a look telling him enough and to cool it. She walked over to Rachelle and placed her hands upon Rachelle's shoulders. They were rock stiff; she began to massage them, but the rigidity never went away. She guided Rachelle back to her chair and rubbed her hand as they sat.

"Your father acts like Job," Pastor Brown said. "You know Job lost everything but never once did he question God's reason. He just waited on the Lord. Dwight did the same thing over the years. He lost Lily and you at the same time, but he kept the faith, no questions asked."

"He never lost me. I jumped into the shoes of my mother, doing everything she would be doing if she was alive. I became the glue." She snatched her hand away, placing them on the chair arms and bracing herself to push into a standing position.

Pastor Brown clasped his hands on the desk; both Zinnia and he waited a moment, allowing Rachelle to take a breath. Zinnia in a voice filled with care asked, "Did you ever take the time to realize you were a child, not your mother?"

Pastor Brown tried to sound a little softer, more reassuring, but it was hard to pull off with his deep boisterous voice. "Don't answer today, but the next time we meet, we would like you to enlighten us with the answer, as well as how could you be more like Job."

Standing Ms. Zinnia pulled Rachelle to her feet, embracing her. "We have been praying for you, Rachelle, and we will continue to do so until the day we die. Remember you are not alone."

Breaking free from the hold of their eyes and Ms. Zinnia's embrace, Rachelle waved goodbye, walking quickly from the office. A stream of tears made their way down her cheeks almost as fast as she was walking.

Zinnia taking a few steps toward the door to go after her, but the power of her husband's voice told her to "Let her go. Give her time."

"Time, she doesn't need any more time," she said as she touched the place where her heart was breaking for a woman she felt was like her very own child. "She's had plenty. It's time for a change."

"It's coming. I can feel it. A lot is about to change."

Chapter Ten

"Dawn, I feel like everyone has been keeping some kind of secret from me," Rachelle said, hanging up a white and black fitted-waistband skirt she'd been holding in front of her.

After leaving the church in haste, she went straight to Dawn's job at a vintage clothing boutique to talk out her troubles.

"Rachelle, you've got to realize, everything is not always about you, nor does it concern you," she said bluntly.

Rachelle's eyebrow rose.

"Do you need to talk about something?" she asked.

"No, Rachelle. I'm just tired of hearing about people keeping things from you, your mother being dead, anything that you didn't place your stamp of approval on. The sun rises and it sets every day. You don't control that, and you can't control life."

"Where is all this coming from? Did I say or do something to upset you?"

"I have parents, too. They live halfway around the world, helping other people and their family. You've never heard me complain nor have you asked how it makes me feel. Not even one time, never ever have you asked." She crossed her arms. "Why? Aren't I your friend?"

Rachelle lowered her gaze as embarrassment swept through her. She hadn't been a good friend.

"You're right. I've been selfish. Do you want to talk about it now?"

"No I don't. It was a point I was making. You're not the only one who has felt pain."

"Alright point made and noted. Now can I ask you something?"

"You just did, but go ahead anyway."

"What's with the hair?"

Shrugging her shoulders, "Nothing really. I wanted to be different, and I wanted a hairstyle matching me, and the type of unbounded naturalness I relish in."

"Then why hide? I would show it off, you're beautiful. You should show the world the real you, not hide behind that cap," waving toward her head.

"Thanks." The little Rachelle said gave Dawn the courage she needed to swipe the loc cap off her head, ball it up, and place it into her pocket. Shaking her locs from side to side and raking her fingers through them, she felt free from all restrictions and secrets. Well, almost all.

Chapter Eleven

Kenyon was finishing up a hatha yoga class. He'd worked all the students really hard this session, promising to be a bit easier the next time they met.

He went into the back, going through a door marked EMPLOYEES ONLY. Stripping off the wet clothes that stuck to his skin, he reached for a towel. As he brought the towel to his face, the door snapped open.

Leigh stood in front of him, blocking the doorway, taking in all his nakedness. From top to bottom and back up again, her eyes drank up his beauty like a woman dying of thirst in the desert, finding a small drinking well.

Kenyon wrapped the towel around his waist and turned away from her prying eyes.

A sly smile curved her mouth at the corners. "Raheem told me to wait here for him when I got here. He said you'd be teaching a class and he'd be in with a client, so to come in and wait. I guess I should've knocked first. I'm sorry for barging in, but I must say," she said, taking a few steps toward him and lightly touching his chest, "I do like what I see, and I'm not sorry for viewing it."

Kenyon grabbed her hand as she began to lower her finger below his belly button, stopping her from undoing his towel. He shoved her away from him.

"Stop it! Step outside until I'm done redressing, please," he said angrily.

Walking backwards, she kept her eyes locked with his. At the door, she grabbed the knob and said in a voice sounding almost like a hissing snake, "Don't keep me waiting."

He released the breath he was holding. As he quickly dressed, Kenyon wondered what Raheem really saw in the walking disaster waiting to happen. He shook his head and laughed; the "ha" and "tha" in the hatha class he taught meant "the sun" and "the moon," exact opposites. Like Raheem and Leigh.

Leigh walked up front to the waiting area, skimming through a health magazine she found on the counter. She was still smiling.

"What do you guys have planned for tonight?" Kenyon asked. She hadn't seen or heard him walking up.

"I um, we um, I'm not sure. Why, do you want to come?"

"Hey there," Raheem saved him from having to answer. "Ms. Smith, I'll see you next month," he said, helping her with her jacket.

"Yes, you will," Ms. Smith said, smiling. "You know I never miss a massage. Or a yoga class."

"Get home safely."

"I will. Goodnight, everyone."

"Goodnight," they said in unison.

Kenyon felt Leigh's unwanted stares, making him uncomfortable.

"If you don't need my help, I'm going to head out. You guys have fun." Grabbing his coat, Kenyon rushed out the door.

"Alone at last," Leigh said, sliding her arms around Raheem's neck.

Lightly he kissed her puckered lips.

Lifting his shirt to his nose, he said, "I need to run home to shower before we head out. I smell kind of ripe."

"You smell strong and manly and even like lavender. We can grab something on our way to your place, and stay in. It's up to you, of course."

"I thought you wanted to listen to some jazz. You can head over there and I'll meet you. I don't want to hold you up."

"I want to spend whatever time we have together. We can dance at your place, alone." Placing kisses all over his face, whining, "Please let's just stay in."

Raheem gently pushed her back, trying to get her attention. His loins stirred. It had been a long time since he'd been with a woman, but Leigh had been making it harder and harder each time to resist.

"I give, you win. Is Chinese food good for you?"

"I was thinking more like some island food. You know rice and peas, fried sweet plantains, brown stewed chicken, and some carrot juice, spiked with a hint of Jamaican white rum. Yum, I can smell the caramelized molasses and the coconut milk." She licked her lips while her eyes rolled in anticipation of the meal that was to come.

"Let's go."

He gave her the money to purchase the food while he rushed home to take a cold refreshing shower. He couldn't trust she would not attempt to join him in the shower if she were there with him. And he couldn't say he would be able to resist her advances. It was best for him to keep her busy while he was naked in all ways.

Chapter Twelve

Tomorrow was d-day. It was now or never. The advice Rachelle had given him was the only thing making sense to Zion. *Don't lose sight of yourself in place of someone else.*

Dinner was not the place to deliver the kind of news he would be dropping on them, but time had run out. He needed to tell them his plan.

The aroma of tomato sauce wafted through all of the downstairs and made its way upstairs, into his nose, awakening his appetite.

"Mom, can I help you do anything?" he asked Zinnia as he walked into the kitchen.

She stood at the stove, sautéing mushrooms and onions to throw into the already bubbling sauce.

Wiping her hands on the apron hanging from her neck, she pulled out all the fixings of a garden salad and homemade salad dressing, placing them onto the countertop of the island in the center of the kitchen.

"You can make the salad and the dressing." Zinnia hadn't skipped a beat. Not even stopping to look at her only child. He was watching her, though.

She was still beautiful even at the age of fifty-five.

He washed his hands, grabbing a knife from the wooden block that housed the sharp cutlery and the wooden vegetable cutting board.

"Mom, when will you slow it down, take it easy?"

"When God calls me home. Until then my work is never done. Plus I need to keep your father and you healthy. I don't know what you're eating behind my back and outside of this house, so when at all possible I got to take care of mine."

"You don't need to worry about us so much," he told her.

Washing off the angel hair pasta with cold water, Zinnia placed three plates on the counter. "One day you'll understand when you have a wife fussing over you and your children. But until the time comes, let me do what I do."

Zachary walked in through the door in the kitchen leading to the garage. "Right on time," Zinnia said accepting the kisses he placed on her cheek.

Shaking his son's hand, he asked, "How's everyone this evening?"

"We're fine. Wash your hands and take your seat at the table," ordered Zinnia.

All that could be heard at the table for the first five minutes was the clinging and scraping of the silverware hitting against the plates.

"How was your day, Pops?"

"Busy as usual, but I wouldn't have it any other way. I love being of service to the people. You'll understand soon. Once you finish school, you can take over some of the duties so I can relax a little. Maybe your mother and I could take a much needed vacation." He winked at Zinnia.

Zion grabbed his water glass, guzzling down the cold refreshing liquid.

"Mom, Pops," he said, looking from one to the other. He placed his napkin in his plate. He'd lost the appetite he'd had.

"I thought you were hungry?" asked Zinnia.

Ignoring her question, he said, "I need to talk to you guys." They gave him their undivided attention. Studying their faces, he knew things would change after he revealed his feelings.

"Go on we're listening," Zinnia encouraged.

Wringing his hands, he said, "Well, I uh, don't know how to say this, but to just say it. I uh-"

"Spit it out, Zion. Whatever it is we can handle it," said Zachary.

"I'll be right back. I need some more water. Do either of you need anything while I'm up? It seems awfully warm in here."

"Zion, sit down. Say what you need to say." Zinnia handed him her glass of water.

"I don't believe I'm doing the right thing." Two sets of eyes, neither understanding what he was talking about. They waited on him to continue on.

"I thought this was right for me, but I was so wrong. I can't do it." He was fidgeting like a little boy. "I made the decision because I knew that's what was expected of me. But I don't have it in me. I don't know what God wants from me, so how can I teach other of his goodness and mercy? I can't mislead people and ask them for offerings to keep a building open. I mean if they want to be in church, they don't need a building for it."

Holding his hands up, Zachary signaled for Zion to stop talking. "You don't want to be a pastor."

Sighing, relief washed over his body. His father understood. Shaking his head side to side was the only answer he could summon.

"Why?" Zinnia asked, placing her fork down.

"I don't think I would make for a good example. I'm confused about the choices I still want to make with my life."

"After all the money we've spent on your education you decide this now. What's changed?" asked Zachary.

"I'm man enough to admit being a pastor is not for me. I can't live for everyone else when I can barely live for myself." He couldn't look at either one of his parents, so he kept his eyes trained on his pasta that was getting cold as the seconds passed by.

"Zion, what are you going to do to support yourself? Where are you going to live?" his father asked. "See, these are decisions you need to make when planning your life. We never looked at you and told you, you had to follow in my footstep. I would be happy if you did, but I would also be happy with whatever choice you made."   "Darling," his mother added, "we didn't realize we placed pressure on you. That was never our intention."

"Mom, it wasn't you guys. It was everyone else. I thought that's what was…I don't know. I didn't want to let you down, but I realize it's not for me. I'm sorry."

He looked from one to the other. The questions were rolling around in his mind what would he do with the rest of his life? His parents wouldn't always be around, and at thirty, he needed to stand on his own two feet.

"We will be proud of you, no matter what you choose to do because we're your parents and we love you," said his father, "but you will have to decide quickly what you plan to do. You have a life to make your own."

Chapter Thirteen

"I told them tonight."

Rachelle listened as Zion recapped play by play what took place with his parents. She held the phone with her shoulders as she searched for the scripture she'd read before praying and going to bed.

"And you were worried. I knew you were worrying over nothing."

"Yeah I misjudged them. I guess it is sometimes better to hear it from a neutral party. I was calling to tell you thanks, and if ever you need anything at all, you only need to call and I'll be there to assist."

"That's what friends are for."

Laughing a boisterous heartfelt laugh, he said, "How cute and cliché, that's a Dionne Warwick song. It's before your time." He tried to suppress his laughter.

"And yours as well. You're only two years older than me silly."

"You make me silly," he confessed.

"How is that so?"

He'd started down a path of confessing to his parents, so it felt right to continue with her. *What could it hurt*, he thought.

"Rachelle, I've known you for as long as my memory serves me. I've watched you hurt, and I always thought it my responsibility to make you smile. Hence my silliness when your around. Raheem is your protector, Mr. Dwight is your provider, or was your provider, but I was and still am your comic relief."

"You left out that over the years you have been and still are a good friend. For that I'm grateful."

For a split second, emotions fogged his mind. She cared for him, he never realized until now.

"Can I be honest with you?" he asked, hesitating. "I don't want to lose your friendship ever."

"I value you as well. I doubt you can get rid of me easily."

Taking a deep breath, Zion said loud and quickly, "I love you, Rachelle. I want to be your protector, provider, and comic relief."

Zion had rendered her speechless. She wondered if Raheem had told him of her life-long secret crush. *No*, she thought, *he would not have done that to me.*

Maybe he did since he's going on to greener pastures, finding Leigh who seems to make him happy. Maybe he's wants the same for me. Rachelle shook her head and focused on the phone. "Zion, are you there? Hello, Zion?" She listened to the silence that answered her and added, "Please, answer me. I know you're there. I will speak to you about this more in person. I won't do this over the phone."

Pressing the power button, she disconnected herself from shared silence, to the worse kind, deafening silence.

As soon as she hung up with Zion, Rachelle sat straight up in her bed and punched in the digits that would connect her to her brother. Her suspicions told her that he had told Zion about her feelings. "Raheem, I thought you were my confidante, my bosom buddy."

"Chelle, what are you talking about?" Rolling over to look at the clock, Raheem read *12:00 A.M.* He groaned; he had a seven o'clock client.

"How could you tell Zion about my hidden feelings for him? I mean it was so long ago. You did tell him-didn't you?" she asked.

"You can't be serious, Rachelle. I didn't tell anyone anything. Besides, that was a high school crush, so long ago as you clearly put it. I'm too old for that kind of game. So are you."

She pressed on with her interrogation. "Then how does he know? Why else would he have confessed his feelings for me? You told!"

Raheem did not have it in him to make her see how easy it would be for anyone to see the feelings both Rachelle and Zion had for each other. Frustration and fatigue built within him; all he wanted was to close his eyes and fall deep into sleep until the alarm clock brought him back to a conscious state of mind.

"Rachelle, you've been unstable for years. Why in hell would I divulge such information to scare our friend? Nobody wants to deal with a chronic mourner. I only do it because I have to."

Rachelle gasped. "This is where you're very wrong," she said, hurt and anger in her voice. "You don't have to do nothing for me ever again."

She slammed down the receiver and took a deep breath.

"I'm not going to cry. No, I'm not going to do it," she said. But no matter how hard she blinked, she could not keep the tears from falling. Rachelle climbed under her quilt and cried herself to sleep.

Chapter Fourteen

Pastor Brown and Ms. Zinnia didn't want to force Rachelle to speak. All they could do was post questions before her and hope she would be willing to respond. Nothing they tried worked. She stared as a zombie at nothing particular.

"Pastor, give me some time with her," Zinnia requested.

Nodding in agreement, he said, "I need to go see the members in the hospital anyway. I'll see you at home later. I won't be late." Pastor Brown rubbed his wife's arm heading before the door.

"See you then."

Closing the door behind him, Zinnia stood with her back up against it. Rachelle hadn't moved a muscle. Zinnia began to pray. "Lord, I need you more than ever today. Use me as your vessel to reach out to Rachelle and understand what she's feeling, what I need to say to reach her in this hour of need. On you I depend, Lord, for alone I am useless. In the powerful name of your son I beg of you. Amen."

Sitting on the edge of the desk, directly in front of Rachelle, Zinnia took her hands, pulling her to her feet and holding her in the comfort of her arms. She said no words, but she loved on her as if she was her own child, humming a calming tune like a mother would for a child who had a nightmare or some kind of scare. Rubbing her back, rocking back and forth, Zinnia held onto her for dear life. She wouldn't let go until something, anything happened.

A deep throated sob escaped from Rachelle. Tears ran down her face; her body shook from the mental pain she felt. She lost another member of her family, while they still drew a breath.

"Let it all out, honey. I got you," crooned Ms. Zinnia.

"He hates me. He was supposed to love me, but he's like everyone else."

Confused, Zinnia asked, "Who hates you?"

"Raheem," she said breathlessly.

Zinnia thought for sure she was hearing things. Raheem always seemed to place her before himself. She had to be mistaken. Maybe delirium had finally taken over her distraught mind.

"I don't know what has happened between you and Raheem, but surely you're wrong about what you're saying. That young man has loved you unconditionally, always."

"Then why did he say such hurtful things to me?"

"Listen, we are to blame for the way you've turned out. But some of the blame is yours as well. You need to look at yourself in the mirror when deciding if you should be a child or a grown woman. Stop acting like a whiny, spoiled brat."

Rachelle gasped. Eyes grew in astonishment. "Yes I called you whiny. You are too old to act like this. Do you have a five year plan? Do you ever expect to get married, maybe have children of your own? We told you about Job when you were last here. Do you think he would have received his many blessings if he complained like you did?"

Grabbing her face, Zinnia turned Rachelle to face her, eye to eye. "Look at me when I speak to you. I may not be who you would like me to be, but I'm the closest thing you'll ever get. Lily must be turning over in her grave right now. Let your mother rest in peace. The Bible says to forget those things which are behind, and reach forth to the things that lay ahead."

"How do I do that without feeling lost?" Rachelle cried.

"You don't have to forget your mother, and you don't have to leave her behind, but you do need to stop using her as a hindrance to move forth in life. Live life and remember she is here with you always. You carry her here," Zinnia said touching the space right above where her heart was beating a steady rhythm.

"Can I share something with you, Ms. Zinnia?"

"Anything."

"I've never told anyone this before. I feel I killed my mother. I remember the day she died, right in this building. It had been Mother's Day. She was so happy and I told her I had a surprise for her. She didn't know I was going to sing her a song," the faraway look returned, bringing a twinkle into her eyes as she went back to that day in time.

It was Sunday morning, Raheem and Rachelle woke up early enough to prepare their mother a big breakfast. Walking out to the garden, Raheem cut two white lilies and four red roses from Lily's serene garden. They'd checked with Dwight the night before and he told them that would be just fine. "Lily would like that," he said.

Rachelle got out the bacon, eggs and pancake mix.

"Rachelle, you making some for all of us, right?" Raheem asked, his stomach was growling.

"After we give Mama her food, I will make us something as well. Pour her a glass of orange juice. I'm almost done."

Raheem took out the silver tray, placing the vase holding the freshly cut flowers and the glass of icy cold orange juice on it. Rachelle finished off their masterpiece with the plate of fluffy scrambled eggs, crispy bacon and mouth-watering pancakes.

Slowly they walked toward their parents' bedroom, knocking softly, entering upon command.

"Happy Mother's Day!" they called out.

Lily was smiling brightly. She was beaming and it had nothing to do with the sparkly shimmer lotion she'd moisturized her body with. Her jet black hair, with a patch of white immediately in the front was untamed. She was so proud of her children for making her breakfast without any help from their dad or her. She knew she was raising them right.

"I knew I smelled something wonderful. You both are the greatest children a mother could ask for."

"Mama, we have a present for you, too." Raheem said, handing his mother a small silver box.

Tears welled up in her eyes as she opened the box slowly. "Having you all in my life is gift enough. You do know that is all I ever need, right?"

They all nodded their heads, keeping their eyes fixed on her face to be able to relish in her joy when she saw their gift.

When she opened the box, Lily sucked in a breath, and the tears fell. "This is exquisite. I love it."

The brooch was a simple, white gardenia. The petals were made out of a stone favoring that of an opal, the form was held together by sterling silver. On one petal, there was a tiny lady bug with its wings open as if it either just landed or was about to take off.

Instead of the choir doing praise and worship, the church had decided to let anyone who wanted to honor their mother in a song or dance to liven up the congregation.

It was Rachelle's turn to give her best performance ever, dedicating it to the woman who gave

her life. As she came onto the stage, she riffed,
sending chills through the people in the sanctuary.
She was singing Lily's favorite gospel song, "Running
Back to You" by Commissioned with a little spin on it
to make it more of her own. Looking over to where her
mother was sitting with her father and her brother,
Rachelle could feel the love, and the meaning of the
song filling her spirit. As she held the last note, a
look of surprise appeared on her mother face; when
she let the note go, her mother slumped over. At that
very second, Rachelle felt a warm rush between her
legs.

"Ms. Zinnia, you were there," Rachelle said.
"You know I ran to the bathroom. I didn't want
everyone to know that I had wet myself, but the joke
was on me. I didn't pee my pants. The very day I
start my period, became a woman, my mother took her
last breath."

Rachelle remembered coming out of the bathroom,
and there was Raheem waiting for her outside the
bathroom. She was so embarrassed; she thought he
could tell by looking at her that she had started her
period. He was there to do what he'd been doing since

then; trying to shield her from whatever maybe too much for her.

She recalled whispering to him, "Go get Mommy for me. I need her now."

He didn't move. Then she realized she hadn't said please. So she tried again. "Please, go tell Mommy I need her to come here. It's really important."

When he still didn't move she had gotten so upset with him. But he tried to keep the tears from falling. As she moved to go get her mother for herself, he grabbed her and told in as calm and as brave a voice as he could muster up, "Something has happened to Mom. She can't come right now."

Zinnia didn't know what to say, so she stayed quiet. She understood now finally. When Zinnia looked at Rachelle, really looked at her, she saw something she hadn't seen in a long time…peace.

"Let's call it a day until next week. I'm sure Pastor Brown will be happy to know you had a breakthrough, and you are almost ready to cross over into the next phase of your life, whatever that maybe."

"Thanks, I feel revitalized. I'm beginning to feel like I'm a part of the living again. A brand new me if you will." Rachelle walked out the office with an obvious bounce in her step, with her head held high.

"Rachelle, one more word of advice." Rachelle spun around, awaiting her message. "Talk to Raheem. It just doesn't seem like him to do such a thing."

* * *

"Hey Zion, I wanted to invite you over for Sunday dinner, and maybe we can go grab some ice cream afterwards. Let me know. Talk to you soon."

Rachelle placed the phone on her desk back into its cradle, fluffed up her hair, grabbed her purse, and out the door she went.

She was ready to step outside her comfort zone, figuring the best way to do it was without procrastination or hesitation. Both of which was likely to make a person stray from what they want. Inviting Zion over was the first step, doing something unexpected was the next. For what she had in mind she needed an accomplice. Dawn fit the bill.

Chapter Fifteen

Kenyon, Zion, and Raheem decided to hang out at the comedy club, Blue Zone. Raheem failed to mention to the others that Leigh would be joining them. When Kenyon was on his way back from the restroom, he bumped straight into her. Seizing the opportunity, she kissed him full on the lips while rubbing up against him in a provocative manner.

There was no denying the hints she was dropping. She wanted him even though she was his cousin and best friend's companion.

"I know you like it," Leigh said, watching as Kenyon eyed her white, low-cut, mini spandex dress. For a burst of color, she wore red pumps that matched the plastic hoops and strings of beads wrapped around her neck, choker style.

"I wouldn't be human if I said I didn't notice what you serve on a see-through platter. But I'm a good and loyal friend, and I wouldn't touch you with a ten foot pole. You're off limits. Your man's over there. Let me bring you to him. Word to the wise, don't come at me that way again, or I will tell him. I have no honor to you."

"Touché," she said walking in the direction he'd pointed

For the remainder of the evening, Kenyon was uncomfortable being around Leigh. She wasn't discreet with her seductive looks; she laid it all out on the table. Raheem seemed to be in another place. He wasn't behaving like his normal self.

"So Zion, I hear you're not going back to school. What's up with that man?" asked Kenyon.

"Nothing really. I need to work on me first before I contemplate delivering messages to others."

"I can understand that. You need to take care of yourself first. I wish some others thought the same." Kenyon looked in the direction of Leigh and Raheem.

"All in due time, everyone finds it in a different moment of their life."

Bringing his cup up to his mouth, Kenyon drained his cola and stood. "I'm out. Zion, do you need a lift?"

"Nope man. I'll catch up with you another time. You alright?" he asked, creases apparent on his furrowed brow.

Kenyon nodded and slid into the stiffness of his black leather jacket.

He waved to the couple and Zion and left. He couldn't help wondering when his life would fall into place.

He looked at how happy Raheem and Leigh seemed, and he wanted that kind of happiness. But then he realized how fleeting happiness could be. He didn't trust Leigh. He wished that Raheem would see her for who she really was. For now all he could do was head in the direction of his own happiness.

* * *

Dawn was sitting on the couch, manipulating metal into abstract pieces of jewelry. A lady had come into the boutique requesting a dozen pieces for the bridesmaids in her daughter's wedding.

Sketching several different designs in her sketchbook, Dawn didn't stop until she came up with the perfect earring and necklace. Elegant enough to wear on the day of the ceremony, but could go perfectly with a pair of jeans and a white top. The wedding colors were the softest yellow and blue. With that in mind, Dawn selected a stone for the center of the necklace made out of yellow glass, the accent side stones were small turquoise beads. The earrings used the same stones, creating a lovely drop-earring.

She had a month and a half to complete all twelve. The job would get her five hundred dollars; two hundred of which she spent on supplies.

The door opened to the apartment, and Kenyon walked in with jacket slung over his shoulder. Dawn was quickly trying to put all her equipment and supplies back inside the wooden box she kept them for safe keeping.

"Are you hiding something else?" He asked already knowing the answer.

"I, um, was putting away some things," she stated cryptically.

"You don't have to hide what you do from me. One this is your place as well as mine, and two as long as it's not illegal, I don't mind."

Sitting next to her on the couch, he picked up her sketching book, flipping through the pages of design after design. Looking up from the book into her face, back down to the book in total amazement, he was unsure of what his eyes were revealing to him.

"Did you really draw these?"

She nodded.

"They're beautiful, and this one here, I've seen you wearing it. Why didn't you tell us this?" he asked.

"Kenyon, we all have things we don't want the world to know about. Well for me I had two things, but well you know how it is," she said shrugging her shoulders.

"No, I don't know how it is. The way I see it you can be the next person with your own line of jewelry. It can be sold on QVC or one of those home shopping networks."

"I couldn't do that. If I did do it and it was successful, I couldn't handle all the orders by myself."

"It would be a lucrative business for you, and that's when you would have to hire a production company of some sort."

"See therein lies another problem, my pieces are handmade, and made with love; if it's with a production company a machine does all the work, and it doesn't have the same feel."

"It would change the lining of your purse."

Dawn thought of the changes she could make with the extra money. She realized it wasn't about the money, but the invigorating feel she got from manipulating one thing to look like something mosaic.

"It's not for me, Kenyon. It's not about the money, either. I like my hobby, when it goes from hobby to a business, the fun is gone."

"How long have you been doing this because you have some skills?"

She started designing jewelry right around the time her parents left her behind. She didn't actually create the actual pieces until she was in her junior year of high school.

"It's been so long, I can't seem to remember," she said, not wanting to reveal that jewelry making came first as a stress reliever, then a fix to her emotional breakdown to being all alone.

"Why am I finding out now?" he asked.

"When I started doing this, I kept out of trouble, then when I told my aunt I wanted to use my talents to have my own business, she said it was a child's fairy tale, and it would not keep food on the table and a roof over my head and to give it up. Rather than giving it up, I kept at it, secretly. No one had to know. I was fulfilled. That's how it's been ever since."

Wiping dust off of his glasses, Kenyon kept his eyes trained on the floor. He didn't want to show the telling signs of someone who understood what it was like to give up hopes and dreams.

He still wanted to encourage her to reach for the stars, if that's what she wanted and desired. "Dawn, do you craft only women pieces, or do you also have a knack for men pieces? I didn't see any men's inside here." He tapped on the cover of her design book.

"I never even thought to try. I don't wear men stuff, but it doesn't hurt to try." Picking up the pencil, tapping it against her face, she stared at a stark white page of her book.

"I can't even think of a thing. I don't know anything about men's fashion or jewelry. You yourself know I don't date much."

"It's no rush. I can help you if you'd like, just tell me what you need and I'll do it. I'd do anything for you. You do know that, right?"

She smiled.

"I'll try again later. It's probably because you're here, and I usually design alone, when I'm deep in thought. I do have one thing maybe you can help me with."

His eyes twinkled with curiosity. "What might that be?"

"Tell me what does Leigh have that would attract a guy like Raheem."

Kenyon was not expecting a question such as that one. He was wondering the same thing, but Leigh was not who he wanted.

"I think it might be the freeness in her spirit. Or the challenge he believes he'll have trying to save her from herself," he reasoned.

"Someone should tell him you can't help those who won't help themselves. On another note, I want to ask you one other thing. It has nothing to do with them, instead it's about you."

"I can handle whatever you ask, I think," he said a little unsure of what she'd ask this time.

"How come I didn't know that you were the twins' cousin? What's the big secret?"

He played with the hairs on his chin. She returned him to a time in his life he'd never want to think about. Here he was digging into her secrets and he had his own. *Fair is fair*, he thought.

Clearing his throat, he tried to figure out where to begin.

"My mom was their mother's sister. My father and mother had a love-hate relationship. They loved to be together, but when they were to together in the same space too long they hated each other. They would fight something terrible. My mother favored Aunt Lily a lot, you know with the skin that looked like it was more cream than coffee, and my father he was midnight black. When I was born I was so light and my eyes were so light, he immediately thought I wasn't his.

"When we came home from the hospital, he beat her like there was no tomorrow, accusing her of cheating on him, but she never did. If he'd taken the time to ask a few more questions before he jumped to conclusions, he would have known there were others in the family with the same eyes."

Dawn felt awful she'd even asked. "You don't have to say anymore. I had no right prying," she said.

He nodded his head yes. He already started and he might as well finish.

"She waited for him to go to sleep, and then she took out her bat, bashing his brains out. Of course since she confessed, his mother ended up with me and Aunt Lily pleaded with her not to keep me away from the other half of the family.

"My mother went to jail and she wasn't in there long before one of his secret affairs beat her to death. So I lost both parents. We never discussed it ever again. It was too hard for my grandmother and Aunt Lily."

"And you too. I'm sorry."

"It's all good though. I know I will never lay my hands on any woman no matter what. I guess I can see what they mean when they say a person doing all the accusing is usually the one doing all the dirt."

Dawn twisted a loc between her index finger and her thumb. In tempo with the rocking of her body, she said, "I guess we all are more alike than we realize. Do you think God knew this would happen to us? Placing us accordingly to be there for each other?"

"I have no clue. It does look that way, doesn't it? Either way I'm glad I have you all in my life."

* * *

Leigh and Raheem stumbled into his apartment, bumping into the table by the entryway; he placed his finger over his lips, silencing the piece of furniture. Even though he didn't smell like alcohol, the glazed look of his eyes was unmistakable; he was drunk.

After Kenyon and Zion had left, Raheem and Leigh had decided to get something stronger than the Sprite for him and Coke for her. It had been so long since he had drunk anything stronger than sweet, caffeinated, fuzzy, bubbly soft drink. He gave free reign to her to choose his drinks. He wouldn't think so the next morning.

Leigh helped him as best as she could to his bedroom, peeling his clothing off, leaving him in his white tank top undershirt and his blue fruit of the loom boxers. She stood back staring down at him, admiring his fit physique. She'd never met a man like him and she admired his respect for women, but wasn't certain he was someone she wanted in her life forever. He could complicate things for her, causing her to feel emotions foreign, yet so natural and comfortable. It didn't seem like forced feelings, but something indescribable.

He definitely was nothing like the other guys she typically went out with. It was hard for her to understand; if a guy like Raheem didn't want her for the obvious reasons, then what was it that kept him coming back for more time with her? She'd tried everything she could think of to get him in bed, none of it worked. Now here he was completely drunk, and vulnerable, yet she didn't want him in this way. He needed to come to her, willingly.

Kissing him lightly on his forehead, she pulled the comforter over him before she left. Raheem made her think about how important she was and should be to herself and everyone else.

"How can I go from uninhibited me to a more pulled together woman, who uses her brain instead of her body to entice men? This I need to know to cross over into a more respectable me," she said, pulling the door close behind her.

Chapter Sixteen

"How are the sessions going with Pastor Brown?" asked Dwight.

"Daddy, how did you know about my meetings? I don't remember mentioning it."

"There's not much about you I don't know. Now are you going to answer my question?"

Rachelle got a goofy look on her face, almost like a child in a candy store. "I'm learning things about me I didn't realize before. But not to worry, Daddy, I'm making great strides."

"That's good to hear, sweetheart." He smiled brightly.

"When are you going to go put your life in order now that I'm on a track to being healthy in mind, spirit, and body? Raheem seems to be in smitten land, and you," pausing for only a quick breath, "Daddy it's time for you to heal, too."

"I'm an old man now, Chelle. I don't have many years left before I go home to glory and my precious Lily."

"Don't say that. You're in the prime of your life, in perfect shape, and handsome for a dad anyway."

"Ok let's change the subject, my life has been full. Now it's my children's turn. Tell me about Leigh and Raheem."

Touching her chest, she said, "Who me? Huh! You know as much as I do. Raheem has changed. Our relationship is not the same anymore. I can't say I'm upset though. Who wants to explain why he's always with his twin sister? He's your son. You tell me what's been going on with them."

"The two of you were always so secretive and no one will ever be able to put a wedge between you. You shared a womb. Don't let Raheem's new relationship destroy what you have had all this time. Life is too short and family is too important. That you know from experience."

Rachelle shook her head. "Daddy, I doubt it has anything to do with Leigh. Something is not right with him. I can't put my finger on it, but after what he said to me a few nights ago, Raheem is no longer my concern. He'll need to come to me and apologize before I will even try to understand what's going on with him. The way it looks, he's tired of me."

Dwight was clearly confused. Those two never had any normal sibling rivalry when growing up. He

was baffled by the eminent rift in his small family.
Deciding not to say anything until he had them both
in his presence, he kept his thoughts to himself.

Trying once again to go to a more positive
note, he asked, "What kind of desserts do you plan on
making for Sunday dinner? You know everyone loves
your fattening desserts, made from love of course."

"Pound cake with a lemon glaze drizzled over
the top. I think that's it."

"Sounds good to me, now let's think about the
rest of the meal."

"Add Zion to the usual diners. I invited him
over."

Looking at her from the corner of his eyes, a
sly grin curved the corners of his mouth as he nodded
approvingly. His baby girl was not a baby any more.

* * *

After finalizing Sunday's plans, Rachelle met
up with Dawn. Today was the day for a complete
transformation. No more dresses to her ankles,
buttoned all the way up to her neck; no shirts
looking like they belonged to her father or brother.
No more closet full of black and white drab clothing,
looking like she could fit in with the Amish women.

Never really looking any men in the eyes, always looking toward the ground searching for things unknown to her and others. After today she would be walking with her head held high and shoulders back in her new high style fashions.

"What should we do first?" asked Rachelle, excitement causing her to bounce her legs.

"This is all about you today. You had my attention the minute you said shopping. But my eyebrows went up when you mentioned haircut. You've never cut your hair, not even a bang when we were growing up. This will be a shocker to us all."

"Dawn, loosen up, and live a little. I can't stay this way forever."

"Alright, well, since you put it that way, start with the haircut. You know so we can find outfits to accentuate it."

"Dawn and Rachelle combed through a ton of hairstyle magazines.

"Girl," Dawn said with a squeaky voice, "This is the one right here." She was pointing to a woman with a sleek looking style, a razor layered cut. "Well what do you think?"

"I don't know if that would look good on me. It's a risky, bold cut." She was beginning to have second thoughts about her transformation.

Dawn knew it. Trying to keep her from backing out, Dawn began reasoning with her quickly.

"You live only once. Wasn't it you who said you can't stay this way forever and for me to loosen up? Think of it like this: it's only hair, and believe it or not it will grow back if you don't like it. Remember, you are ready to step out on faith, and live a little, even if it is risky."

"What if I look stupid?"

"You can't live through what ifs. If you're always worrying about the outcome you can't control, then you'll never do anything fun and exciting."

A woman walking up from the back with spiky, platinum, blonde hair approached them. She had on a pair of fuchsia Crocs to brighten up her rather dismal attire of black pants, black shirt and black smock. Her name tag looked right at home on the left breast pocket, displaying the name "Melody" written in a calligraphy type.

"Hey ladies. Which one of you is Rachelle?" she asked in a voice that didn't quite match her appearance.

Dawn pointed in Rachelle's direction. She had to give her a little nudge to get her to respond.

"Oh yeah, that's me," Rachelle said, a nervous chuckle escaping her.

Extending her hand, Melody said, "There's nothing to be afraid of. I'm Melody and I promise to take good care of you. Here at Hairstyles by Design we operate like one big happy family, and the clients are cousins from out of town."

She began leading her away from her friend.

"Rachelle, I will start checking out the different outfits, which will cut down on some of the time."

"Ok. I'll call you when I'm done."

Melody led Rachelle to her station. She ran her fingers through Rachelle's rich auburn tresses, checking out the healthiness of the hair shaft and her scalp.

"Who does your hair normally?"

"I do," Rachelle answered with a question lingering in the background.

"What did you have in mind for today?"

"I don't really know. All I do know is I've been wearing my hair like this for as long as I could remember. I want a change, something to wow people with, having certain individuals taking a double take."

"Are you by chance trying to get a certain individual's, attention?" Melody asked staring at Rachelle's face in the mirror waiting for an answer. She didn't miss the dreamy look on her face.

"I already have his attention. Now I want to keep it."   Throwing caution to the wind, she showed Melody the picture of the style Dawn thought would fit her perfectly.

Melody looked from the picture to her and back to the picture again. "Can I make a suggestion?"

"Sure, you're the professional."

She took the magazine and placed it in the basket on the floor, and said, "Let me do what I do. I don't like that style for your oval shaped face, but I do know the one that will have you staring at yourself all the time. Best of all, I'll keep it simple."

"Work your magic."

* * *

For two hours, Rachelle was pampered. While under the dryer she decided to go all out and get a manicure, pedicure and have her eyebrows arched.

Melody hadn't allowed her to look into the mirror; all attempts she tried failed. "Call your friend before I reveal your new image to you. I want both of you to see it at the same time," Melody told her.

Not even trying to put up a fight, Rachelle did as told. Pulling out her cell phone, she dialed Dawn's number.

"Hey girl, I'm done."

"Ok, meet me-"

"No, no," Rachelle interrupted. "You need to come back to the salon. I haven't seen my hair yet, and Melody won't allow me to see it without you. Now hurry up and get down here. I can't take the suspense anymore."

Closing her phone, she put it away as she admired her fingers and her toes. She had never been one to go to a salon, but the relaxed feeling she got from allowing someone else to have the responsibility of making her into an eye catch, not an eye sore.

Dawn came running into the shop. Melody was at the counter waiting for her. Stretching her hands out in front of her, palms facing Dawn, she said, "Slow down. Now when we get closer to where Rachelle is sitting, I want you to close your eyes. I want you both to see her new look at the same time. Ok?"

"Fine with me, let's go. Don't let me trip over anything."

Melody led the way; halfway to the back she informed Dawn to close her eyes tightly, helping her along the rest of the way. The large mirror on the wall had a black drape covering it, used in times like this. She stood the two friends side by side; she grabbing the cord to pull back the drape and said, "One, two, three, Dawn, open your eyes."

Rachelle wanted to touch her hair, but didn't want to mess it up. Melody had given her a Chinese bob.

"This style is really easy to maintain. You can either wrap at night, combing it down in the morning and go; or you can comb it down and bump the ends under with a curling iron, a flat iron will work really well also. Now if you want to take it to another level, flip the ends up and you will be the talk of the town. What do you think?"

Rachelle looked at Dawn, waiting for her to say what she thought first. Although she would never admit it aloud, it mattered to her what people thought of her, especially those close to her.

"I like this one better than the one I chose. You look so beautiful." Dawn was tearing up.

"You better not make me cry," Rachelle said. "Melody, I love it. Thank you so much for fitting me in and doing such a great job."

"I'm glad I could be of assistance to a new you. Call me when you need to come back again," she said handing her a business card the color of her Crocs with black writing.

Checking every mirror she walked by, Rachelle smiled remembering what Melody told her.

"What are you smiling at?"

She told her what Melody had said. They both agreed she was absolutely right with her prediction.

They completed the day with six shopping bags filled with clothes and two filled with matching shoes. When Rachelle was alone in her bedroom, she looked at her image in the mirror attached to her dresser, thinking, *I have the hair, the clothes, and the shoes. Now all I have to do is keep the man.*

Chapter Seventeen

"Excuse, who are you and what have you done to my daughter?" Dwight asked the back of Rachelle's new 'do. He took her by the hand and spun her around, admiring the all grown up version of his daughter.

She was wearing a knee-length black dress with a belted, form-fitting olive blazer. She had on little make-up, some eyeliner, a neutral lip-gloss and silver eye shadow, accenting the blazer.

"Do you have an interview? I know today is Sunday, but you are dressed to get the job."

She could feel her face getting warm. The compliment made her smile. "Thanks, Daddy. Are you about ready to go to church? If not I'll go ahead and see you there."

"I'm ready. I want to be there when people start asking who the gorgeous sister is on the stage, singing praises to God. I want to be able to pop my collar and say that's my daughter. You look beautiful, honey. You remind me of what your mother looked like when I first met her."

Rachelle was beaming now. She'd heard many times before that she favored her mother, but never had anyone ever told her she looked or reminded them of her mother.

"Let's go before I can't sing because I have this goofy grin on my face because of you."

* * *

Parking in their normal spot designated for the members of the choir, Rachelle checked her appearance once more in the mirror before exiting the car. Her hair bounced with every step she took. When she turned to look at Dwight, her hair fanned out around her head, landing back in place, not a strand out of place.

"Daddy, if you see Dawn, remind her to save me a seat, please. I've got to get to the choir room."

Dwight didn't get a chance to respond; she kissed his cheek and off she went down the hall.

She made it in time to warm up with the other members of the choir, all of who couldn't keep their eyes off of her. They all said a prayer to be able to touch someone through song. Before she knew it, one by one the others in the room were taking turns complimenting Rachelle on her makeover.

All of this attention was so new to her; it had her floating on cloud nine. Rachelle walked out on stage when the band began playing, hoping to help someone feel as good as she was feeling. She was ready to lift up her voice in praise to an awesome God, the one who had given her another chance to have happiness in and around her life.

Lord, you're so good and your mercy endureth forever…

Each song seemed to lift the whole congregation's spirit more than it usually did. It was a Sunday when Pastor Brown was going to allow Ms. Zinnia to preach.

"Good morning, brothers and sisters. It's so good to be back in the house of the Lord for yet another day. And for that," she paused "we should praise the Lord."

Flipping open the Bible on the podium, she continued, "Turn in your Bibles to Matthew six verse thirty-three and thirty-four. Let us read it together."

The congregation read: *But seek first his kingdom and his righteousness, and all these things will be given to you as well. Therefore do not worry about tomorrow, for tomorrow will worry about itself. Each day has enough trouble of its own.*

Zinnia took a sip of her water and looked down at her notes before moving on. "Some of you may be wondering what things will be added to your life if you give your all to God. I'll tell you what those blessings are: clothes, food, a place to live, how about knowing you will be in place with great happiness?

"Worrying will not allow you to be a servant to God; it's a hindrance to your life. It blocks the many blessings you are entitled to. The Lord placed every one of you on this earth, his earth to fulfill a purpose. That does not include thinking about this from the past you cannot change or the troubles of a few hours ago. Live for the moment, and whatever comes tomorrow you will deal with it then.

"Don't walk around lost. Pray to God, ask him to take the burden, leaving you with the time to enjoy life to the fullest. Enjoying life is a blessing."

Throughout the sermon, all that could be seen from every row of the sanctuary was heads nodding, agreeing with a timely message for many under the roof of Abiding Grace Tabernacle. Sitting there Pastor Brown was praising the Lord for showing him early on in life his calling to minister to the community. Showing them there was a way even when there seem like all hope was lost.

"Grab your neighbors' hands, repeat after me. Say neighbor, don't give up, stay quiet and listen. You're important and have a purpose, and only God can tell you what that is. I have faith in you and most of all, so does the Lord."

Applause erupted; praise the Lord and halleluiah could be heard throughout. Pastor Brown approached the podium, closing the service in prayer.

As she gathered her belongings, Rachelle was showered with kind words on how she looked from the other churchgoers. But her mind was on the message she had just receive. She had spent a long time thinking of how she wanted her mother back and the cruelty life had dealt her. Ms. Zinnia had confirmed it was time to leave the past in the past and to forge ahead.

"Rachelle, you look good," said Kenyon. "I mean you've always been pretty, but now I'm going to have to watch you like an overprotective brother."

Dawn rolled her eyes. "Don't start acting like Raheem," she said.

"He doesn't have to worry about that. Raheem could care less what happens to me."

Dawn and Kenyon exchanged glances; for them this was a first. Rachelle hadn't told anyone except for Ms. Zinnia and Dwight about the changes in her relationship with her brother.

"I know you got a new look, but remember we've been there long enough to know how you two operate," Dawn said. "He's protective of you, and you don't want him to show any affection, give any attention to anyone else, but you. So we're not buying that mess you selling."

"Wow! You've got us all figured out, don't you. Well, you'll see I've turned over a new leaf. I have a different person in mind, and that person has nothing to do with my brother. Did you guys see my dad? We came together and I'm ready to go home."

"Nope, haven't seen him today."

"Me either," Kenyon chimed in. "Dinner is still scheduled for today, right?"

"Yes, like it always have been. Zion will be joining us this evening."

"That's great. Did you need us to bring anything?" asked Dawn.

"Nothing but yourselves."

Rachelle waved. Dawn and Kenyon turned to see who she was waving at. They saw Zion heading their way.

"Hey there," Rachelle said, trying to restrain herself from touching her hair.

"I almost didn't recognize you. You look great," he said, eyes wide and taking in all the changes.

"Thank you." She blushed. "Are you still coming over for dinner this evening?"

"I wouldn't miss it. Can I help with anything?"

"No, Dad and I have it under control."

"Ok, then I will see you all later."

"Bye," they all said. Rachelle followed him with her eyes until she could barely see the back of his head.

"Oh I get it now. I wonder does Mr. D. know you are going after Zion. Maybe I should tell him."

"Tell me what Kenyon?" Dwight asked, walking up behind him.

"Why Rachelle got it going on all of a sudden."

"Shoot, boy, what you mean all of a sudden? My baby girl has always been a beauty, from her head down to her little toe, since the day she was born."

"If you say so, she had a couple of iffy years when we thought she'd be special looking."

"Boy, don't make me band you from Sunday dinner."

"Mr. D., you wouldn't do that, would you? I mean I'm a growing man. I need all the nutrition I can get."

"Don't test me. I know taking food away from you is like a whipping." Dawn and Rachelle laughed. "Plus you know how to cook, so you wouldn't be starving, which brings me to my next question. When will you make a meal for all of us? You can use our house since your apartment isn't going to hold everyone."

"I asked if we could help, but Rachelle said no."

"No, Kenyon, I asked if we could bring something and Zion asked if he could help; you didn't ask anything," Dawn reminded him.

"I knew that meant me, too. See you all acting funny with me because Rachelle had a makeover and you…well look the same."

"See, that there is going to get you Thursday's leftovers. I need to go dig it out the garbage can."

Another round of laughter came from the ladies.

"Daddy, let him have his fun. I don't mind his slick remarks. He can eat dinner, but let's not give him any pound cake. Today he can have fluff out the jar."

Kenyon stayed quiet, not taking any chance when it came to missing out on Rachelle's tasty cakes.

"We need to get going, Daddy. We'll see you all later." Rachelle and her father began walking away arm in arm.

* * *

Silverware could be heard hitting the dishes in the dining room. Once again Raheem showed up unexpectedly with Leigh in tow. Leigh looked great, but Raheem was a sight.

He looked as if something or someone had beaten him with full force. They all stared at him. The shock on Kenyon's face was the most obvious because he had last seen him Friday at work and the person sitting in front of him now did not come close to the person he worked with.

"Leigh, I really like your earrings," Rachelle said.

Automatically, her hands moved to touch the dangling chain of gem stones hanging from her ears. She'd found them in a pawn store. It cost her a whole week's worth of tips, but she didn't care; she liked them a lot.

"Thank you."

"When are you going to come and hang with the A.R.T.S.? You should've already been out with us since your friend is a member," Dawn said.

Forehead creasing, Leigh looked at Raheem, but he didn't seem to notice her looking at him. "What's the A.R.T.S.?"

Kenyon said, "Awaiting a Relationship through the Spirit. It's the singles ministry from the church. You don't have to be a member to attend."

"She doesn't need to be at the A.R.T.S. meetings, gatherings or whatever you want to call it. She isn't single," said Dawn.

Rachelle shoved more food in her mouth trying to keep her thoughts to herself. Dawn however couldn't restrain herself.

"Leigh, are you married, engaged or in a committed relationship? If your answer is yes to any of these, then fine we understand why you wouldn't be able to hang with the rest of us. Since I know you and Raheem have been spending time with each other a lot lately, I hear a no on the horizon.

"I also remember the time I called while you were there and you answered telling me Raheem didn't seem to be feeling well, so you were leaving to go home. Surely if your relationship was anything other than pure acquaintances, you would've stayed. I wouldn't have had to come over to take care of my friend."

"That's how you ended up in-" Raheem stopped mid-thought. He hadn't stopped wondering what had transpired that night, resulting with Dawn and him being in his bed without their clothing.

"Ended up where?" asked Leigh. "We are more than just friends who hang together. We're making big plans, but those plans will change depending on the answer to where did Dawn and you end up, Raheem?"

Keeping her eyes averted and trained on the plate in front of her, a quick thinking, fast talking Dawn answered, "We were outside in the park walking when I got tired of moving and trying to hold on to a staggering man. We sat down on a bench, and I guess I didn't know how tired I was because I dozed off right along with him."

Leigh tossed the explanation around in her head; after a few minutes, she decided the response sounded believable, continuing with the conversation without so much as a quizzical glance in either Raheem or Dawn's direction.

"You mention something that happened in the beginning of our relationship, but Raheem and I are planning for our future."

"Sounds lovely," commented Rachelle. "I didn't realize it was anything more than a friendship. You and I should hang out sometime since you seem to be getting close to him." Sarcasm dripped from her words. She knew Raheem; he had never been serious about anyone. *This obsession won't last*, she thought. *And I will be here once Leigh is gone like all the others.*

"That would be nice. Maybe all of us could get together again, but instead of eating in, maybe some dancing. I just love dancing." Leigh's face had brightened with excitement.

Meanwhile, Raheem had been staring at Rachelle from beneath hooded eyes. Dwight, never missing a beat, addressed his son's demeanor.

"Are you feeling ill, Raheem?"

He shook his head.

"Your eyes are red and heavy as if you're catching the flu or something."

"I couldn't feel any better than I do now if I tried to. It must be my allergies."

"You've never had allergies a day in your life. Maybe it's something else like fatigue, possibly something you smoked or drank," said Dawn.

"How would you know, Dawn?" Raheem asked. "You don't know about everything that goes on here just because you're my sister's friend. Don't think I missed the other slick stuff you slipped in there. I heard you…we all heard you. You have a lot of nerves."

"Almost as much as you have coming up in here inebriated by Lord only knows what, claiming to have allergies," said Dawn with a triumphant smirk curving her lips.

Rachelle took that as her cue to go get the dessert. She needed this meal to end quickly. Knowing how she was, she didn't know how much longer she would be able to bite her tongue. Even if it was only to concur with Dawn; Raheem was not allergic to anything but the truth.

"Excuse me, does anyone want anything else besides cake while I'm up?" she asked, taking the napkin off her lap and standing.

Everyone gave a negative response. She took her plate with her. Unbeknownst to her, Raheem grabbed a couple of plates as well, following her to the kitchen.

"Did I do something to you?" He startled her when she heard his voice. "You haven't said two words to me all evening. That's not like you at all. You're usually talking up a storm. What's gotten to you?"

Rachelle didn't acknowledge his presence, as much as she wanted to yell at him. She wanted him to apologize, to be the caring and loving brother she'd known him to be. But at last she couldn't bring herself to respond to his ongoing array of questions.

She didn't need him saying more hurtful things, especially not while others were in earshot of their conversation.

"Rachelle, do you hear me speaking to you? You change your appearance and now you're too good to speak to me. Is that it?"

She began singing, a Yolanda Adams song, softly, "Quietly he speaks to me, gently he leads me. Lovingly, the good shepherd carries me. He carries me safely in his bosom."

Raheem grabbed her by the arm, spinning her around to face him. "Rachelle," he said her name forcefully, "why are you acting like you don't hear me?" His nose flared, brows creased, and his jaw muscles clenched tightly.

Speaking her words carefully, and slowly, almost as if she was afraid she would say the wrong thing. No mistake could be made about the certainty her voice projected when she said, "Take your hands off me now."

The intensity in her eyes matched the power in her words. He released her arm.

"I don't owe you an explanation at all. I don't even have to speak to you if I chose not to, but what

I do know is I am no longer your concern. Lord knows I don't want to burden you with my whiny woe is me rants and complaints."

Raheem was dumb-founded. He had no clue as to what she was talking about. He couldn't remember saying anything offensive to her.

"Excuse me, I have to get back to my friends and family, those who I matter to."

"I don' even understand what's going on with you. You haven't said two words to me all evening."

"I believe I've said more than two words a moment ago. Are you happy now? Remember the world doesn't spin on your axis, only you do."

Side stepping him, she returned to the dining room. He wasn't going to drop the subject that easy. "I wasn't finish speaking to you."

"I was done with you though."

"You can be so stubborn at times. What do I mean at times? You've always been difficult to deal with. But who was there all along? Me," he said beating a fist on his chest. "Now because I have a life that doesn't revolve around you, you shut your trap like a clam. You've never shut me out before, never."

"Maybe I don't want to be an open book anymore. Maybe I've finally grown-up and only want to think of myself. Maybe I don't want to worry about anyone or anything except for me, and whoever I end up with. Just maybe I want to be selfish for once in my life."

"Wait a minute. This is about him?" Raheem asked, pointing to Zion. "Is he the reason why you're behaving this way? Are you seeing him now?"

He had done it. Raheem had succeeded in embarrassing her in front of Zion and everyone else. She pushed her chair under the table, trying to keep as calm as her raging mind would allow her to be. She exited the room, heading straight for the front door. Rachelle grabbed her coat from the closet to the right of the door, and went for a much needed walk to clear her mind and quiet her nerves.

People driving past her were bound to think she was a crazy woman because she was talking out loud to herself.

Chapter Eighteen

Dawn sat outside Raheem's apartment in her car, waiting for Leigh to leave. It was all too clear; Raheem had issues, which needed to be addressed. She couldn't help but feel as though the situation wouldn't have gotten out of hand if she hadn't commented on Raheem being drunk again.

It was for that reason they had ended up in a less than ideal situation. She had to tell him once and for all.

She looked up from her sketch pad just in time to see Leigh coming out his building getting in a white four door sedan; she couldn't tell what kind of car it was. Dawn waited until she pulled off and was out of sight before she left the safety and comfort of her car.

"You forgot something, baby?" Raheem asked as he opened the door. The smile drained off his face when he saw Dawn standing on his doorstep. "What do you want? I'm too tired for anymore games and arguments." He still hadn't moved out the way, allowing her passage into his domain.

"We need to talk. So you can either invite me in or we can air out all of our business right here loud enough for your neighbors to hear."

"What business do we have?"

"Why don't you ask your next door neighbor about the noise they heard a few weeks back? I'm almost positive they will remember my voice."

He slid out the way quickly. He'd been wondering what took place that night.

Dawn took a seat on the couch and Raheem walked over to the entertainment center, cutting off the music. Taking any sounds that may place thoughts of any unwanted situations to occur, away.

"You're acting like you're afraid of me. I don't bite."

"Why are you here?"

"Because you should be thanking me for saving your hide earlier. Imagine what your light bright honey would have done or said if she knew you were with me."

He had to sit down, his head was spinning. His worst nightmare was coming true, sobering him up. He hated to but he had to ask. "Why didn't you stop me?

I'm sure I wasn't that intoxicated where I wouldn't understand no."

She smiled devilishly.

"Why would I do that? Raheem, like Rachelle with Zion, that's me with you. I've always wanted you, but for some reason you never noticed me. Here I was all this time under your nose, in front of your face, and you go get Leigh."

"So what are you saying?"

"I'm glad you were drunk. When I called and Leigh answered, I was so tempted to hang up, but I wanted to talk to you for a second. Even if it was to allow you the opportunity to blow me off, but she said you weren't feeling well and couldn't come to the phone. At first I was going to call Rachelle and tell her, but I know she can be overbearing with her nurturing complex. I decided to come and check on you myself."

"Ok I got that, but how did we end up in bed together without our clothes?"

"At first I had no clue you were drunk, but I got you out of your pants and shirt. Once I had finished, you did the same thing to me. I didn't put up a fight, I already told you why. One thing led to another and we wound up in all sorts of compromising positions."

No relief sigh; in its place he was breathing rapidly. "I always saw you like a sister; I kind of feel like I slept with my little sister."

"Too bad that's how you see me. I can offer you so much more than a person walking around as lost as ever. I mean does she even know what she wants to be when she grows up?"

"Why do you always do that?"

Not sure she knew what Raheem was talking about, she asked innocently, "What did I do? It seems like every time I'm around you or I mention Leigh's name at all, you say I did something wrong. Is that even possible?"

"You always find fault in everything she does. You need to look at yourself and see what faults you have. Maybe you're the reason why your parents are in the Philippines indefinitely."

His comment hurt Dawn as if he had punched her in the stomach. She grabbed her thick red sweater and her keys. She said one last thing to him over her shoulder before leaving. "I don't know who you are anymore. Ever since you started seeing Leigh you've been changing slowly but surely. You so busy worrying about me and mine, why not take a look at you and yours, mainly your sister. You might learn something from her."

* * *

Zion had looked for Rachelle for ten minutes, but he was unsuccessful in finding her. To him and the others present, it seemed like they were watching strangers interact. Everyone called it a night immediately after Rachelle left; no one wanted to be at the receiving end of Raheem's unexplained fury.

He didn't bother returning to say goodbye. He went on home, hoping he would be able to have a good night's rest. Not being able to find Rachelle and comfort her made him a bit uneasy.

When he entered the house, he saw the light on in the kitchen. At the kitchen table he found his mother with her eyes closed and her right hand on a book. She looked peaceful.

"Hey, Mom," he kissed her on the top of her head. "What are you doing?"

"Reading the daily word before I drink my nightly glass of warm milk, and then I'm off to bed."

"Your message was awesome earlier. I know it made a lot of people think, me included. Now I know what Rachelle said to me is true."

He had her full attention now. Zinnia turned the chair she was sitting in to look at Zion; her eyes were asking the question she didn't speak.

"She told me to pray for direction and then be still and listen to God's instruction."

"She's one wise young woman." Zinnia smiled.

"That's part of the reason why I like her. She wears her heart on her sleeves and is wise, but not cocky with it. She's different."

"She has an old spirit about her. She's making great progress in the sessions."

"Really? I know you can't tell me exactly what was said, but has she said anything about her and Raheem? I'm worried about them. Something is seriously going on between them. I know for certain after what happened tonight."

She exhaled hard.

"What happened?" she asked revisiting in her mind the last session.

"Rachelle wouldn't even look at Raheem, let alone speak to him. He was determined to make her acknowledge him and it exploded from there. It was like she was trying to avoid him and he purposely crossed her path, saying the key things to make her madder. Did she say anything at all about them having a disagreement?"

"I'm not at liberty say. You need to discuss this with either Raheem or Rachelle." Zinnia hates not being able to tell him, but her oath to the people who came to see her were important.

"Mom, please. A head nod will do. I need to be able to do something, but how can I know if you don't help me?"

"Zion," she had that look on her face, signifying she meant business, "I told you to speak with them. You know I can't give you anything, but if you are a true friend, and really concerned, then take your concerns and go be a friend."

"Thanks, Mom. I understand. I'll figure this all out by myself."

* * *

Dwight was sitting in the family room waiting for Rachelle; she'd been gone a long time. He knew the fresh air was good for her, so was the time alone. He jumped from his seat when he heard the locks releasing from the chambers.

To him she still looked angry. Dwight stood before her blocking her way. Needing to reassure her, but not knowing what to say, he opened his arms leaving the silence in place. Rachelle walked into his comforting, consoling embrace. It was what she needed to cool the flames raging within her spirit.

It was yet another change in her life she had no say or control over. For years, Raheem had been the comforter and protector, and Dwight was her provider. Now she provided for herself, and her father crossed over into the shoes Raheem used to wear. She could feel his love warming her chilled body due to the elements outside. She hung on to her father as if her life depended on it.

She broke the silence, with her head still on his shoulder. "Dad, how did Raheem and I get to a place where we disagree so much?" For a fleeting moment, she was his little girl again.

"You're both changing, steering your lives into different directions. People change all the time, but family should and will always stay the same. Of course over time there will be additions through marriages and births; nonetheless, it's still family. You know what else? It's ok to have disagreements, but it isn't ok to harbor ill feelings, especially when the person who did the hurting," he paused, tilting Rachelle's head up to look him directly in his eyes, "doesn't realize what they have done."

"How could he not know? He's not dumb."

"And neither are you, but you know the man that sat in this house, at that table, with us this evening, wasn't the person we know and love. Something is going on with your brother, and you need to forgive him and move on because right now it will take his family to save him."

"I'll think about it. I'm going to bed."

Dwight stood at the bottom of the steps, watching her retreat into the solace of her bedroom.

Chapter Nineteen

"Good morning, Rachelle."

"Hello, Ms. Zinnia. How are you this morning?" Rachelle asked her.

To Zinnia, Rachelle didn't resemble anything like Zion had described the night before. She seemed to be very happy.

"I can't complain at all. Just excited about this time of year, you know, Thanksgiving being a week away, and then Christmas and the start of the New Year. Plus, I like to eat, if you couldn't already tell by looking at me." Zinnia ran her hands down along her sides while laughing.

"I like this time of year also. All of my friends and family come together. I don't know if it will be as good this year, too many unusual things going on around me."

"It doesn't have to be that way. For a matter of fact that's why I came to see you, I want to have a session with you. I know it's not our usual day, but I feel as if this is that important. Pastor Brown is waiting for us in his office. He wants to share something with you."

"Ok, I'll be there in a few minutes. Let me get someone to cover my desk."

"Never mind that, any calls that come in can go to the voicemail."

Rachelle followed Zinnia into Pastor Brown's office.

"Rachelle, you look so graceful. I see leaving you in the care of Zinnia was good for you. She has that kind of effect on people."

Rachelle smiled, but didn't say anything. She could only wish to have someone so proud of her that their faces lit up.

Zinnia pulled out the two chairs in front of the desk, gesturing Rachelle to take a seat.

"I know you're wondering what I wanted to speak with you about," Pastor Brown said, leaning on the desk, hands folded under his chin. "I wanted to teach you something important without telling you what it is because some lessons are better learned if you find it out by yourself."

"Alright, I'll do my best. I'm listening."

"The story we want to share with you is about when Zachary decided he wanted to take charge of his own ministry, begin his own church," said Zinnia. "I was working a part time job over at the library. I knew we couldn't live off of my one little check."

"I had to quit my day job in order to be accessible to the parishioners. I couldn't tell them I can't visit you in the hospital until the weekends because I have to go to work. I did what I needed to do," said Pastor Brown.

"Ok, I don't quite get what you're telling me."

"I'm not done yet," answered Pastor Brown.

Rachelle leaned back in her chair.

"I had a lot of work ahead of me. The two most difficult parts were finding a place as well as a name."

Zinnia eyed Rachelle carefully, assessing her level of understanding. "I'm certain you're aware of what a tent revival is."

Nodding her head, Rachelle said, "Of course I do. Everyone has seen one."

"That's what Pastor Brown started out with. It only made sense to encompass the word tent in the official name of the church."

Rachelle tilted her head slightly, creases forming on her brows. "Tent isn't a part of the church's name."

A deep throat chuckle rose out of Pastor Brown. "It is, while it isn't. Tabernacle is derived from the Latin word tabernaculum, which means tent."

"Isn't that awesome? The day he chose the word tabernacle, I'd been reading from the book of Exodus, chapter twenty-five verse eight that states 'And let them make me a sanctuary; that I may dwell amongst them.'"

Pastor Brown and Ms. Zinnia were smiling big, but Rachelle was not sure what they were getting at.

He tried to make his point clearer without telling her word for word what he was driving at. "Now you already know the Lord works in ways unknown to man. I had a Jewish friend I was sharing my thoughts and ideas with. Sometimes I wanted an unbiased opinion on the things I was doing, trying to not stress Zinnia out with all my crazy ideas. He told me that in Hebrew a tabernacle was known as Mishkan, which translates to a residence or a dwelling place."

"So, your friend confirmed what you were already doing?" Rachelle asked. "Zinnia, dear, I don't think I need to say anything else. She understands."

"She certainly does. Our paths were written before we were born, even the person we will end up with." Zinnia and Pastor Brown exchanged a quick look. "Whoever it is has to be on the same page as you. They need to see your vision as if it were their own. The choices are there for us, but it's up to us to choose the road that will lead us to Christ.

"He never leaves us alone. Now I know you're dealing with some issues with Raheem, but what path have you decided to take? Nothing is ever easy because Zinnia and I struggled for some time. But one thing is for certain, we abided by the faith we had in God. We placed all our trust in him."

"I get what you're saying. I know what I need to do."

A few moments later, Rachelle walked out of the office with a new challenge in mind.

* * *

"Hey." Zion had been waiting at Rachelle's desk for her. "How are you doing today?"

"I'm doing wonderful," Rachelle replied. "What brings you here, handsome?" She tilted her head and played with the heart charm hanging from the silver necklace around her neck. She was flirting with him. It was something new for her, but she liked it.

Licking his lips, that seemed extremely dry all of a sudden, he replied, "I wanted to take you out to lunch because I think we have some unfinished business."

"I would love to join you. Any place special you want to go?"

"DeMali's, of course." Grabbing her purse from the bottom desk drawer, she said, "Let's go, and I want dessert, too."

"Anything for the lovely lady." He smiled.

They enjoyed a delicious meal of fried chicken, blackened tilapia, mustard greens, baked macaroni and cheese, and potato salad while engaging in a light and airy conversation. Zion watched until Rachelle had her warm peach cobbler and scoop of French vanilla ice cream to complete a delectable mouthful of goodness. He watched as she placed a few spoonfuls into her mouth, feeling a bit jealous it wasn't him.

"So you wanted to share your feelings about the way you see me in your life, face-to-face," Zion said. "I'm all ears."

"First, I need to ask one question. Did Raheem put you up to this or tell you something?"

Zion was puzzled by her questions. He'd never held a conversation with Raheem about her. "No, he hasn't said anything. Should he have?" He watched her closely, but her facial expression only got softer.

She shook her head while a smile crept onto her lips. "I wanted to be the one to share with you how I've felt about you for years."

He leaned on the table, propping his chin up with his hands. "And exactly how is that?" he asked, feeling warm and tingly.

"I have always had a crush on you. It was great that out of all of the males we hung around you were not an option for anyone else, but me. I wondered why you never asked me to the movies or any proms. But everyone realized I had it bad for you."

"I didn't think you were ready to forget taking care of everyone else and being mine completely, so I waited. No I never noticed because you treated all of us the same. You were like a mother hen." He chuckled.

"Is that a bad thing?"

"Not really. I know I shouldn't be selfish, but I wanted most if not all of your attention on me and me alone," he said.

"Oh really?"

Zion nodded.

"I'm ready now, how about you?" Rachelle asked.

He beckoned for her to come closer with his finger. She did as told. Zion braced himself with one hand while he tilted her chin up with his other, placing a soft electrifying kiss on her lips.

Trying to stay composed, he asked "How's that for an answer?"

She hadn't quite recovered from the chills she was feeling from the kiss. "Are you going to answer or keep staring at me with that goofy grin?" he asked, still waiting for her to answer.

"I like your way of answering. I can get used to that."

"Me too, but we will take it slowly. Is that alright with you? I don't want to rush anything and get it wrong. I want it all to be just perfect."

"Anything you say," she said. "As long as I get to be with you."

"Hey you two, what brings you here?"

Looking up, they saw Leigh smiling at them.

Rachelle smiled brightly, genuinely excited to see her.

"Leigh, I'm glad we ran into you. I guess I forgot you worked here. Well, anyway I wanted to call you, but I didn't have your number. I guess I could have called here, but like I said it slipped my mind," she rambled.

"Hey take a breath," said Leigh. "What did you need me for?"

"Sorry. Um, when would it be good for us to go out and have some fun? You know do some girl things?"

Leigh happily said, "Whenever you want. Let me know."

"Great." Going into her purse, Rachelle pulled out a little notebook and scribbled her number down, giving it to Leigh. "Call me later and we can set something up. Ok?"

"Sure. You guys a couple now?" Leigh asked being nosey.

Zion and Rachelle exchanged knowing glances. They hadn't gotten that far into the discussion of taking things to another level. She waited on him to answer while he waited on her to do the same.

"Y'all don't have to answer, but I know a couple when I see them, especially when I saw a public display of affection not long ago."

They all busted out laughing. They couldn't deny it if they tried. Anyone watching them could see the emotions one felt for the other. If Leigh hadn't interrupted when she did, Zion was certain he would have kissed Rachelle again, but this time a little deeper than the last.

Chapter Twenty

Soft Hands was very busy today. The phones had been ringing not stop all day. Kenyon and Raheem spent the last hour returning all the messages for the day.

"That's it for me," Kenyon said. "I believe we need to decide before the week's end on what we're doing for a receptionist. We can't keep operating in this manner, it's unprofessional."

"I told you we should hire Leigh," said Raheem.

"I see you're still being irrational with your one track thinking."

"Maybe you need a lady to be around so you can understand why I need to be near Leigh so much."

Kenyon took off his glasses and cleaned them. The person for him would come along in due time.

"Ask Rachelle if she is willing to give up her position at the church to help out family."

Raheem looked at him as if he didn't know him. "I don't think so. She's been acting strange ever since she changed her appearance."

"Dude, are you kidding me? You really need a wakeup call or something. If you haven't noticed, you've been acting differently. It may be due to whatever substance you're abusing."

Raheem was doing some quick thinking. Yeah he'd had a couple of drinks lately, but nothing to concern anyone.

He decided playing dumb was the best thing to do right now. "I have no clue what you're talking about."

"Sure you don't. It's probably because you can't remember the stupid things you said and did on Sunday."

He tried hard to remember, but the only thing coming to mind was the conversation he had with Dawn. She said the same thing about his behavior. Nothing about Rachelle came to mind. He hadn't spoken to her in awhile and that was so unlike her, but he was so used to her calling him and checking in with him. He rarely ever needed to call her.

"What did I do?" he asked realizing there had to be some truth to what was being said because Rachelle wasn't the type to turn her back on family.

"I love you and all, Cuz, but you need to call Rachelle and find out from her. You two were already showing signs of having tension between you before we started eating. You snapped when she wouldn't speak to you."

Scratching his head, Raheem thought really hard but still nothing. "I don't remember doing anything wrong."

"That's when you know you have a problem, when you can't remember. Ask your sister."

* * *

Kenyon was standing by the bar waiting to order a soft drink. His back was to the stage. Someone rubbed up against him. When he turned to look, there wasn't anyone there he recognized. He chalked it up to someone passing by the cramped space.

As the bartender placed his lime infused Coke in front of him, once again someone rubbed up against him, but this time their hands reached around his waist, holding him very tight.

Grabbing the delicate hands invading his personal space, he spun around asking, "Do I know," the last word a mere whisper.

There standing before him was Leigh. She looked fabulous. The green eye shadow on her lids accentuated her sparkling brown eyes. The outfit she wore left nothing to the imagination; it was a smoky gray velour pants suit. It clung to every crease and crevice.

Sucking his teeth, Kenyon turned away from her and took a long swallow of his drink.

"Aren't you going to offer to buy me a drink?"

"Why would I do that?" asked Kenyon.

"That's what a true gentleman would do," she said, staring at him from beneath hooded eyes. "You are one who knows how to treat a woman properly, right?"

"Now how would you know that? I've never been with any woman in your presence."

"I see the way you treat Rachelle and Dawn. I want you to treat me just as good and better," Leigh said seductively, drawing a line down his chest with her finger.

"You must have lost your mind. Either that or you are completely drunk."

"No I just know what I like and want and I go for it."

"You're unbelievable," Kenyon said, shaking his head. "Raheem is my cousin and best friend. I don't cross that line, no matter what."

"I'm not married to him. We simply hang out together, nothing more to it than that."

"Didn't you tell us about you and him talking about the future?"

She laughed. Not a nervous laugh, but one that said you got me there.

"Is that all you can say?"

Shrugging her shoulders, she picked up his glass, seducing the rim with her tongue, before taking a sip. "What's there to say? I know you've checked me out already tonight. I don't understand why you won't give in to me. They always do."

"Leigh, go home and take a cold shower. You really need it. And for the record, I'm not a part of they, just a part of a great friendship and family."

He dropped a few dollars on the bar and headed for the door.

Dawn was sitting on the couch reading when Kenyon came in slamming the door, startling her.

"What in the world?" she asked, clutching her chest. "What's your problem?"

"I don't understand what Raheem sees in her. I mean come on already, by now he should be ready to tell her to kick rocks."

"I presume you're talking about Leigh."

Dawn watched him throw his keys onto the coffee table and his jacket next to her on the couch; she knew Kenyon was madder than she thought.

"Calm down and tell me what happened."

He was now pacing behind the couch. Still not a word emerged from his mouth.

"How about I make you a cup of chamomile tea to calm your nerves?" she asked not really waiting for an answer.

As if talking to himself, he mumbled, "How do I tell Raheem she keeps coming on to me? I refuse her even when she's rubbing up and pressing up against me, sending chills up and down the length of my body. I avoid looking at the second layer of skin she calls clothes because only a fool wouldn't notice. But she insists on seducing me."

"Kenyon, it's obvious that Leigh is who you're talking about. If she really did all those things, you need to tell Raheem. And if he won't listen at least your conscience is clean because you told him.

What he does with the information is none of your business."

Shaking his head, he said, "But you don't understand. I can't hurt him in that way."

"You hurt him more if you don't tell him. But it's up to you, because if you don't tell him…I will."

Chapter Twenty-One

Leigh and Rachelle planned to go shopping for the Thanksgiving dinner that would be taking place at the Martin residence. It was crowded at the local Shop and Go, but Rachelle still needed the things to make seafood lasagna, sweet potato casserole, and green bean casserole, which would accompany the other traditional dishes she had already began prepping.

"Are you going to help me with the cooking, especially since you work at DeMali's?"

"I'm just the waitress. They don't let me near the stove."

Rachelle laughed.

"You didn't learn how to cook in the group home?"

Leigh looked at her like she was crazy.

"They barely wanted to provide us with a meal that was edible and you expected them to teach us how to cook? Are you always this naïve?"

"Naïve?" asked Rachelle shocked by Leigh's comment. She knew she tried to think in a positive manner about the things she didn't know about, but she never thought of herself as being naïve. "It was only a question. Never mind, it's all good. Do you know how to make anything at all?"

"Kool-Aid and boxed macaroni and cheese. Oh yeah and a Betty Crocker box yellow cake with white frosting," she said sounding all proud of the little she knew.

"I see why you work at DeMali's, to keep from wasting away."

Desiring a different topic besides her lack of culinary skills, Leigh thought of something else they could talk about.

"What's going on between you and Raheem? Have you made up?"

Rachelle rolled her eyes. The last person she wanted to talk about was her brother.

"We're fine," she lied.

"You sure? Because Raheem told me last night he wasn't sure how he'd make it through dinner with you acting different. So did you talk to him this morning or something?"

"No, but we're family, Rachelle said, becoming frustrated. "It'll work itself out." She took extremely deep breaths as she counted in her head.

"If you say so. I don't want to see my future family fighting or having any type of rifts. Did your parents fight?"

Rachelle took a few more breaths. Leigh was touching on almost every nerve in her body with her choice of conversation pieces.

Remember you're trying to save your brother from the person he's turned into, ever since he started dating this simple minded girl, she told herself.

The holidays were already a difficult time for her without speaking about her family. She didn't want to have to deal with the sense of loss and being unthankful because she didn't have her mother.

"If they did, we didn't know about it. They never fought in front of us."

Leigh was in shock. She remembered the foster homes she stayed in for a short while; there always some type of fighting going on; not enough money, dirty house, staying out late. The foster mothers were always arguing with their husbands about them eyeing their meal ticket.

"Have you ever been around arguing?"

Rachelle laughed. *Talk about naïve*, she thought. Leigh was pretty naïve for a girl who grew up in the system.

"I didn't say I lived a sheltered life. We didn't experience arguing in our home, but there were disagreements which led to lengthy discussions. Plus we went to public school so we have seen our fair share of fights and such silly antics."

"So if you discussed things, why won't you discuss with Raheem what you're upset about?"

Leigh had fed Rachelle her own words. They were hard to swallow. She didn't have an answer.

"I think I have everything I will need," Rachelle said looking at the items in the cart while trying to ignore Leigh's question.

Leigh had returned back to the memories of past holidays. If she was with a family, she didn't ever enjoy any of the holiday festivities except to clean-up after the family had eaten because foster care money didn't allot for these types of lavish dinners. Anything you could find in a can was all there was to eat.

After a while, holidays became another day with the same daunting chores and bland meals. However, once she became a permanent resident of the group home, they provided them with turkey, baked macaroni and cheese; albeit runny, and the other fixings of a festive dinner. For Leigh, something was still missing, someone and someplace to call her own.

"Leigh, earth to Leigh."

Refocusing her eyes, Leigh saw Rachelle staring at her, along with the cashier and the others in the checkout line.

"Why is everyone staring at me like that?" she asked innocently.

"Because," Rachelle replied, "I've been saying your name for a few minutes now. Where did you go?"

Waving her off, Leigh said, "Let's go. I was just standing here day dreaming."

Eyebrows going up, Rachelle's curiosity was piqued.

"Are you going to share?"

"There's nothing to share. Nothing…at all."

"I'll drop it for now," Rachelle said as she took the bags from the cart and placed them into the trunk of her car. "Will you come to church on Thanksgiving morning to help feed the homeless?"

Anxiety filled Leigh's body. Homeless people scared her. She had placed the idea in her head that the reason her mother gave her away was due to her being homeless. Leigh never wanted to believe her mother had her and gave her away just because. That would mean she was less than trash because at least one person's trash was another's treasure, and no one ever wanted her.

She didn't even understand why Raheem wanted her. Being so used to men using her and leaving, she wanted to hurt him before he got the chance to. Leigh knew eventually Kenyon would get sick of her advances, and go tell Raheem, causing him to leave her. The thought of being alone again caused a solitary tear to make its way down her left cheek.

Rachelle witnessed it. She embraced Leigh, whispering to her, "I don't know what it is, but I'm here."

Rachelle didn't want to pry, but she realized there was more to Leigh than she was willing to see before. Now she wanted more than ever to get to know and like her even if Raheem was out of the picture.

Chapter Twenty-Two

Raheem hadn't been expecting anyone. He knew Leigh for some reason would be hanging out with Rachelle. When the doorbell rang, he was startled.

Ever since they found out about Dawn's locs, she seemed more open to allowing others to see them. She was standing at his door, her locs pulled into a chignon. Under her wool pea coat, she was wearing a crocheted dress, which clung to all her curves.

Raheem found himself checking her out from head to toes, unconsciously licking his lips.

"Are you going to let me in or continue to drool over me?" Dawn asked, a sly grin warming her face.

He stepped out of the way, allowing her passage into his space. He rested his back on the closed door, remembering the morning he'd awakened to her nakedness in his bed.

"What you want, Dawn? Why are you here?"

Spinning around rapidly, Dawn looked at Raheem as if he were a stranger.

"I thought we were friends. What has happened to you?"

She took her coat off, making herself comfortable.

"I mean you meet this, that, hell I don't know what you call her, and she's got you so wrapped up in her, you've forgotten who you are. What's the deal?"

"I don't know what you're talking about. Leigh is fun to be around. I'm simply enjoying life a little more than I ever have. Is that a crime?"

"Yes it is," Dawn said in a matter-of-fact way. "It's especially bad when you're mistreating the same people that have been there for you and loved you."

Raheem shook his head.

"You're blind, Raheem. Leigh is making you into a fool."

Dawn paused.   She wondered if she should continue telling him about what Kenyon had told her.

He mocked her body language.

"Do you feel left out? I have a life which doesn't include you and so does Rachelle."

He laughed at her.

That was the worst thing he could have done to her. Dawn wanted to hurt him, too. Without any further thinking she said, "What you going to do with Leigh once you realize she's not into you? I mean if

she was," she shrugged her shoulders, "she wouldn't
be after Kenyon. Now would she?"

"Wh- what are you talking about?" he asked, his
eyes narrowing to slits.

"You heard me loud and clear. She's been coming
on to Kenyon like buzzards on a recently dead
caucus."

Raheem paced the length of the room. Dawn sat
looking at her nails. She smirked at the thought of
him turning to her in his time of distress. Rachelle
wasn't there for him, and he couldn't go to Leigh.
She was the reason for all his anguish. That left her
or so she thought.

Attempting to drive her point home, Dawn said,
"I'll tell you what your problem is."

Raheem was still marching back and forth. Dawn
got up from where she was, walking in front of him,
blocking his way.

"Listen to me."

Raheem stared into her eyes. His brown eyes
were piercing right through to Dawn's soul.

She continued on since she had what seemed to
be his undivided attention.

"You need a God-fearing woman such as myself. I know the things you need to make you happy, and you won't ever have to worry about me and anyone else."

He tried hard, but he couldn't hold it; Raheem burst out laughing right in her face.

Out of breath, while still trying to suppress the laughter, he said, "I knew that was your problem. You want what you can't have. You're no God-fearing anything. If you were, you wouldn't have been so eager to sleep with me."

"Christians have sex, too, Raheem. Or did you forget your parents didn't find you lying in a manager?"

"I got all that, but you need to understand there's nothing you can offer me. Been there, done that, and it wasn't memorable to me. So I'm guessing it wasn't all that either."

As her anger level escalated, Dawn's breathing became irrational. Her plan wasn't going liked she had hoped.

Raheem wasn't finished.

"Even if you were the last woman on earth, the only way I would touch you again would be if I had a few drinks in me. Maybe even something stronger."

Dawn got her coat and headed for the door. She needed to get away from him before the stream of tears appeared. She refused to give him the satisfaction of knowing he'd hurt her with his words.

As she reached the door, Raheem threw out one more insult.

"You'll never be as good as Leigh is, no matter what God you serve."

Chapter Twenty-Three

Rachelle pulled the front door open swiftly, trying to quiet the unexpected visitor before they woke up her father.

"What in the world is the—" The rest of her question stayed in her mouth. The sight of a crying Dawn silenced her and calmed the anger that was building within her.

"Come on get in here and warm up. Tell me what's the matter," Rachelle said leading Dawn through the kitchen to the sun porch. "Is someone hurt?"

Dawn shook her head no.

Rachelle walked into the sunroom, grabbed the blanket off the back of the lounge chair. She wrapped Dawn in it. Rachelle ran her hands up and down the length of Dawn's arms, attempting to warm her.

"I can't help you if you don't tell me what's going on," Rachelle said. She stared Dawn in the eyes, but she still remained silent except for the occasional sob.

"I'm going to make you some tea. It will calm your nerves."

Rachelle left Dawn alone. While she was gone, Dawn looked around the room. She saw the things she's always wanted, but couldn't have other than by way of friendship with Rachelle.

The Martin family quilt was on the back of the wicker love seat. The years of love was felt when wrapped in it.

The table they usually used for dinners in the sunroom had been moved inside to hold the desserts for the Thanksgiving dinner. The empty space where it usually sat caught Dawn's attention. It's exactly how her life felt, like there was a big empty spot.

Being around Raheem and Rachelle filled the yearning for family a little, but now she wanted a family of her own. Dawn always imagined Raheem and her would one day be husband and wife and parents to their own children. But after his behavior this evening, she wasn't certain that would ever happen.

Rachelle came back carrying a steaming cup of chamomile tea. The subtle smell triggered Dawn to immediately take a deep cleansing breath. The message on the cup was perfect for her. *Let Go & Let God.*

Rachelle waited patiently for Dawn to take a few sips. She watched as Dawn closed her eyes. Each swallow calmed her a little more.

"Now tell me what happened and what I can do," Rachelle said touching the center of her chest, "to make it better."

Dawn looked at the liquid in the cup. The light contrast of yellow and green was as calming as the smell and taste of the actual tea.

"You know I love coming here," Dawn began. "Mr. Martin has been the best male role model ever." Rachelle nodded. "He really cares about you and Raheem and anyone who comes in contact with him."

Rachelle smiled. The tension she felt in her jaw eased a bit as she thought about the loving man she had as a father.

"Yea, Daddy is great."

"You're lucky. I don't know what that is like. It's been hard over the years for me to know I have a father and mother who believes it was God's wish for them to be apart from their only child. I sound selfish right now, but—"

"Dawn, honey, that's not being selfish. You know me of all people can relate. It's only recently I stopped asking why."

"Well your mother died and that was not her choice. Leaving me here was their choice." Dawn clutched the handle of the cup tighter. "What mother would pickup and just leave their child for someone else to raise while taking care of others?" asked Dawn, the bitterness evident in her voice.

Resting her hand on Dawn's left thigh, Rachelle said, "I can't answer that."

"All I've ever wanted was a loving family. And tonight those dreams were thrown against the wall and smashed to pieces."

Tears made a path along her nose to her lips, disappearing between the top and bottom thickness.

Rachelle squeezed Dawn's thigh. It was an attempt to get her to look in her direction. When Dawn turned, the sadness and dread took the glow from her skin, leaving it dull and flat.

"Dawn, you don't look so good," Rachelle said.

"Do you think you'd look better if you finally realized no matter what you did you would never be with those you really want?"

Rachelle was so confused.

"I don't understand these riddles you're talking in."

Dawn turned her head, looked Rachelle in the eyes and said, "I'm saying Raheem doesn't want to be with me. And nothing I do will be good enough to get him to love me."

Rachelle's mouth hung open. All these years she never knew Dawn had feelings for Raheem.

"How do you know all of this?" asked a shocked Rachelle. "Did he say something to you?"

Dawn's sarcastic chuckle made Rachelle jump.

"The question is what he didn't say."

"I'm so sorry, Dawn, but you knew he and Leigh were getting close."

Dawn laughed.

"Yeah sure they are, if he wants a third person in their relationship."

Rachelle was having the hardest time tonight understanding what Dawn was talking about. She'd never seen her this way before.

"Who's the third person?"

"Kenyon."

Rachelle's eyes widened. Dawn had to be lying.

"Put your eyes back in your head. Leigh has been making advances toward him. Even though he's been ignoring it, he felt bad about what she was doing behind his back. He told me and I tried to handle it. But instead Raheem handled me."

Neither Dawn nor Rachelle noticed Dwight was standing in the doorway listening. He saw how sad Dawn was and turned, heading to his son's apartment to straighten him out. He'd had enough of the mess Raheem was dishing out.

Chapter Twenty-Four

Leigh hadn't been at Raheem's apartment thirty minutes before there was a loud knock at the door.

Raheem didn't budge.

There was another more urgent knock.

Leigh looked from him to the door. She got up from the seat right beside him, shrugged, realizing he wasn't going to be the one to see who it was trying so desperately to get in.

Cracking the door a little bit, Leigh peeked out to see Dwight standing with one hand on his hip, the other holding on to the doorframe. Seeing him, she pulled the door completely open, stepping aside to grant him entry.

"Good evening, Mr. Martin."

"How are you, Leigh?" he asked not looking at her but at his son slumped down on the couch.

Dwight scanned the living area; the things he saw disturbed him as much as his son's drunkenness.

Keeping his emotions completely off his face, Dwight turned finally looking at Leigh.

"I look forward to seeing you bright an early day after tomorrow. But at this moment, I need to have a heart to heart conversation with Raheem."

Dwight glanced over his shoulder quickly and back to Leigh.

"Quite honestly it may get ugly in here. I don't want you to see that side of me."

Dwight helped Leigh with her jacket. She walked over to Raheem kissed him on the forehead.

"Call me later," she said.

Dwight was waiting for her at the door. As she crossed the room, he pulled the door open.

"Are you okay getting to your car alone or do I need to walk with you?" Dwight asked.

His thoughtfulness brought a smile to Leigh's face. She felt a lump ease its way into her throat.

She cleared her throat trying to push the lump down. "No Mr. Martin, I'm good. See you Thursday."

Before she could finish waving, Dwight had the door closed. He walked over to the coffee table picking up the four empty beer bottles and a Grey Goose bottle.

Raheem barely lifted his head to acknowledge the presence of his father. He placed his feet on the table in the spot where the bottles were sitting moments before.

Dwight looked at him and felt enraged; this couldn't be the man he had raised. He walked over to Raheem and kicked his legs off the table, causing Raheem to jump up.

"Man, Pops I'm not in the mood tonight for this."

Dwight nodded. "Oh, yes, you are." He walked right up to his son's face and poked him in the chest. "You ought to be ashamed of yourself. You mother would be so disgusted to see you like this."

"See me like what? I'm living," Raheem said as he fell backwards onto the couch.

Stretching his arms wide, Dwight looked around. "Is this what you call living? What has come over you?"

"I don't see you having any problems with Rachelle's transformation, so why you have a problem with mine?"

Dwight laughed.

"Boy you can't be serious. Rachelle is not the topic of discussion here…you are."

Dwight grabbed Raheem by his left arm, yanking him up off the couch.

Trying to free himself from his father's grasp, Raheem stumbled.

"If you think I'm letting you go, think again. I am going to sober you up quick fast," he told him as he dragged him down the hallway to the bathroom. "I want to make sure you hear me loud and clear once I start talking."

Dwight turned on the shower full blast. Not bothering to undress his son, he pushed his head under the stream of ice cold water.

Screaming, Raheem said, "Have you lost your mind? Get off me, man!"

"I will stop when I feel like it. I will not stand around and let you destroy your life for some girl you just met."

"Leigh makes me happy."

Dwight pushed more and more of Raheem's body into the shower. He was mustering all the strength he had left in his body to hold his son under the water until he was back to his senses. After what seemed like ten minutes, Dwight let his son go.

He took the towel from the rack and threw it at him. "Now I'm only going to say this once to you."

Raheem slowly looked at his father with squinted eyes.

"I don't care who you want to spend your life with, but when you start hurting others, that's when we have a problem."

"Who am I hurting, Pops?"

"The people who have been there for you all your life, and I won't sit down and watch as you destroy them."

Raheem didn't know who his father was talking about. Yes, he had a disagreement with Rachelle, but that wasn't anything for his father to worry about.

"You can stand there and look stupefied," Dwight said, "but you know what I'm talking about. You need to think about."

He nodded in agreement. His head was beginning to hurt as his buzz from binge drinking began to wear off. He knew if he agreed his father would back off and at the moment that's all he wanted.

As Dwight headed for the door he spun around quickly, facing Raheem, and tripping him up.

"What now?" Raheem asked. "I heard you before."

"Pick wisely who you want to give your heart to."

"I'm only dating one person, Pops."

"That might be true, but there has been someone in love with you for years and you need to let her down without crushing her spirit completely."

Scratching his head, he wondered if his father had had a little something to drink as well.

"I don't know who you talking about," Raheem said.

Dwight threw up his hands. "You want to play dumb, I'll tell you then. Dawn has always been in love with you."

Raheem looked puzzled.

"Dawn!"

Chapter Twenty-Five

Thanksgiving morning found Rachelle in the family kitchen preparing all the desserts. She needed them to be out of the oven, leaving room to prepare everything else. Once she got the turkey into the oven, she would lie down for a couple of hours, before doing anything else. Rachelle would leave her father to keep an eye on the turkey while she rested. They were expecting the usual guests with the addition of Leigh.

Rachelle thought back to the conversation she had with Dawn the night before last. She hoped that it wouldn't be uncomfortable with the two of them being in the same room; the atmosphere was already tense with her and Raheem being around. She didn't like the changes she saw in him ever since he met Leigh, but she couldn't say anything because that is who he opted to be with. She couldn't judge her; Rachelle had her own demons to deal with.

"Good morning, Rachelle. Why didn't you wake me so that I could help you?" asked her father. He placed a kiss on her forehead while reaching around and dipping his fingers into the cake batter she was pouring into the pans.

"Daddy, I wanted one of us to be rested. Later on I won't be that good of a hostess because I am tired already." She put the pans in the oven, then reached for her glass of ice water and took a long swallow. "You can watch the cakes and then put the turkey in once you take them out. I'm going to take a shower and then take a nap for an hour or so."

"Ok, sweetie. I'll be here. When is everyone due to show up?"

"I told them three o'clock, which of course means we won't eat until four. No one ever arrives on time." She tried to stifle a yawn as she headed for the stairs.

As soon as her feet hit the bottom step, the doorbell rang. She looked at her watch; it was only ten o'clock. Her father came rushing out of the kitchen, shooing her up the stairs. "You go on up. I will entertain whoever this is."

"Ok." Another yawn escaped from her lips.

Dwight opened the door to see Leigh standing on the other side. "Good morning, Leigh. You're a bit early for dinner, but that's alright. Come on in." He held the door open for her. He took her coat from her and placed it in the coat closet.

She hadn't said a word yet.

"Can I get you some coffee or some juice?"

"I'll take some juice, any kind that you have."
She followed him into the kitchen. "Thank you."

Pointing to the kitchen table, Dwight said, "Go
ahead and take a seat." Reaching inside the
refrigerator, he pulled out a bottle of cranberry
juice. Rachelle insisted they keep it in the house at
all times to keep their kidneys intact. Dwight smiled
as he poured the juice, realizing how much his
daughter was like his loving wife. Always doing
what's best for those they loved and cared for.

"What brings you here so early, young lady?"

"Well, um." Leigh took a sip of the tart drink.
"I was hoping I could help Rachelle prepare the day's
meal. I mean I know I'm not that good at cooking, but
at least I could chop or mix something."

Dwight stared at the fair skinned young lady
wondering exactly what was it that his son saw in
her. She was not at all what he had expected Raheem
to fall for. They were so different.

"I'm afraid Rachelle got up this morning and
did mostly everything already. All that is left to be

done is putting the turkey in the oven, once I take
out the cakes."

Leigh looked a bit let down. She stared into
her half full glass of juice, rubbing her fingers up
and down the glass wiping at the frost forming.

"What's the matter?"

"I was hoping that I could spend sometime
getting to know Rachelle a little better. I know how
close knit this family is. And since Raheem and I are
getting closer, I really want to try and form some
sort of a bond with his sister."

Dwight didn't see Leigh fitting in to easily
with Rachelle. She was tough to get close to. She
took care of the men in her life since she was
fifteen. Leigh had a better chance of getting to know
him and maybe then a closer connection would form
between Rachelle and her.

"I hope that you will have a chance to get to
know Rachelle. And even if you don't stay with
Raheem, I hope you will still be around. We tend to
learn from each other."

"Thanks."

Trying to keep the conversation going, Dwight
asked, "What's your goal in life? I know you work at

DeMali's as a waitress, but surely you don't want to work there forever."

Leigh looked confused. No one had ever taken the time to ask what she wanted out of her life. All the foster families kept her for the money that the state gave them and used her to clean their homes. But never once did anyone take notice in her as more than just a maid and a meal ticket.

She shrugged.

"Don't do that," Dwight scolded her as if she was one of his children.

"Don't do what?"

It was at that very moment the realization of how innocent Leigh really was hit Dwight. She was still a child a lost one at that.

"Use your voice that God has blessed you with." He looked in her face, waiting for her to look him in the eyes. For reasons unknown to him, he felt the need to nurture her as he did with his own children. "Look at the person who is speaking to you. It's rude not to pay attention. You also make yourself seem inferior to those around you."

"Oftentimes I am."

"Oh, but I beg to differ. You are not beneath anyone. You deserve all they have and more. That's the way you need to think."

The timer on the stove chimed. "Excuse me a moment. I need to get those cakes out and the turkey in."

Dwight walked across the room, busying himself with the task Rachelle had left for him to do. He hoped that Leigh would take that time to think about what he had just said to her.

He whispered a quick prayer for God to use him to place Leigh on the right track. Thank Him for leading her to them so they can show her the way.

"Sorry about that, young lady."

"Not a problem. Can I ask you something?"

"Sure you can. If I have the answer I will give it to you, and if I don't, I will find it for you." Dwight clasped his hands together and waited for her to ask whatever was on her mind.

"Y'all are so in tuned with God." She paused to look up into Dwight's face. "Can you tell me if there really is a God, why did he let my parents go away and leave me in the hands of people who cared nothing about me?"

She had caught him off guard. He was thankful he had said that quick prayer a few moments before because this was a tough one. He had heard the same questions asked by Rachelle and Dawn, even Kenyon had asked it a couple of times. The only one that never spoke those words of doubt had been Raheem. *That might be the reason behind Raheem acting out of character lately,* thought Dwight. He made a mental note to address Raheem and his lack of connecting with his emotions.

"That is difficult to answer. But there is a God. Did your parents die?"

"No."

"Now think about it. You're not certain what kind of life you would have had if you stayed with your parents. But the people who took you in were the ones that may have had ulterior motives, but they did open their homes to you."

Leigh wasn't buying it. "I eventually couldn't stay with anyone because of the husbands. Their wives were afraid they would be tempted by my…my body. So I spent my last few years as a ward of the courts in a group home. Where was my blessing in that?"

"You survived it all and lived to tell your story. You met others who lost their parents just like you, but are still living their life to the fullest." Dwight thought about the transformation that Rachelle only just made.

"I guess I can't believe in a man I can't see and those parents I couldn't see either. I don't know maybe one day."

"I can take you to church. It's never too late to learn about God and why we love Him so." Dwight waited for the response to his invitation, but Leigh didn't respond. "I'm not sure why Raheem didn't invite you to church."

"Oh he has. From the first day I met him he asked me." Shaking her head, she said, "I haven't found the reason why I should go as yet."

"For solace and understanding" came the answer from behind her. Rachelle had walked up on their conversation. Leigh turned to face her.

"Hey, Rachelle, how are you?"

"Good morning Leigh. You need to connect with God to heal your broken spirit. He doesn't take the ones we love away to hurt us, but because he has a bigger purpose for them and they are needed up in heaven."

Leigh didn't expect Rachelle to be the one to tell her all of this. She simply wanted to be friends with her. But she listened intently.

Rachelle pulled out the chair beside Leigh, taking a seat and facing her. "I have my good days and my bad days. The good ones are when I think of my mother smiling down on me because of the choices I have made. A scent of some kind that reminds me of a time that I shared with her, appreciating each other's company.

"The not so good days are when I want to ask God 'why did you take my mother from me, before I was ready?'" Rachelle's eyes seemed glassy from the tears pooling. "If and when I get married I will not have my mother there to give me words of wisdom or to help me get dressed. But who am I to question God and his doings?"

Dwight recognized the hurt Rachelle suffered with from time to time. He too had those good and bad days, for different reasons. They were being selfish with their thoughts, but then again they wouldn't be human if they weren't a little selfish at times.

He reached across the table and touched both their hands, then said, "Holidays are a time to get together with friends and family. Today is Thanksgiving and we should be giving thanks for the people we still have, the memories of those we once had, and the future we will have with those still around us and those to come. Let's not focus on the sad parts of life, at least not today."

Rachelle got up and went to check the turkey. She didn't need Leigh reminding her that she was missing her mother today.

"Oh give thanks, unto the Lord, for He is good, for he is good," sang Rachelle. She was trying to stay in a good mood. The holidays were especially difficult for her.

Every holiday Rachelle and her mother used to get up early while the guys slept in and get the meal going. They baked pies, chopped vegetables, and seasoned meats with flour on their faces and songs in their hearts. They enjoyed each other and that's what Rachelle wanted to keep in mind during the holidays. Her alone time to reminisce about the good old days is why she got up so early to prepare the meal. She felt the presence of her mother in that kitchen each and every time.

Leigh's eyes widened as she watched and listened to Rachelle sing. "You sing really beautifully. I've never known anyone who could sing that good."

Rachelle stopped singing immediately.

In an attempt to alleviate any bad feelings Leigh may be having, and to get Leigh off the subject of her singing, Rachelle said, "Hey Leigh, did you want to help me with the cakes? I need to get them out of these pans and onto cake plates."

"Sure." She jumped out of her seat and ran over to the sink and washed her hands. As she dried them on the dish towel sitting beside the sink, she watched Rachelle pulling out the cake plates. She rinsed and dried them.

"The cream cheese frosting goes on the chocolate cake, the lemon goes on the vanilla, and the cheesecake gets the slice strawberries. Now jump in and let's get this done." Rachelle looked over her shoulder at Leigh. "By the way Leigh" she waited for her to look up, "thank you for the help. I appreciate it."

Chapter Twenty-Six

Leigh and Rachelle had a little while with each other before the others began arriving. The first to arrive was Pastor Brown, Zion, and Ms. Zinnia. Zion was carrying his mother's peach cobbler and a carton of vanilla ice cream.

"Happy Thanksgiving!" said Dwight. "Come on in here and sit down."

He was happy to be surrounded by his dear friends of so many years. They were the only family that he really had left aside from the twins and his nephew.

"What can I do to help?" Ms. Zinnia asked as she kissed the cheeks of everyone in the room. When she got close to Leigh, she offered her a hug. Leigh's back straightened like a board. She didn't expect nor was she used to this type of greetings. She was more of a wave or handshake girl.

Rachelle smiled at her from behind Ms. Zinnia. It was of her way of telling her it was alright. That smile coming from Rachelle helped her to relax a little more.

"Ms. Zinnia, you can relax. Leigh was nice enough to volunteer her time early this morning.

Together we got everything done before you got here.
I don't think I scared her too much, so maybe she
will help me with the future holiday meals.

Leigh looked surprised. She didn't know how
long she would be welcomed because once they realized
she came with issues, she figured they would want her
gone. She felt a warm tingle creep over her body just
knowing she was welcomed with no strings attached. No
expectations that seemed hard for her to deliver,
just her simply being who she was and trying to find
who she wanted to be. *Thank you*, she whispered.

"Where is everyone else? You told me three,"
said Zion.

"I know, honey, but we're talking about the
late bunch. They should be here in a few."

Rachelle nor Zion had realized that their
parents sat, watching them interact with each other.
They had all silently prayed that the two would one
day find their way to each other. They had a
connection since childhood, but with Rachelle
grieving for all those years she could never see past
the tip of her nose or outside the family home.

The door opened and in walked Raheem. He wasn't
clean shaven as he usually was but he was dressed

impeccably. "Happy Thanksgiving, everyone. Sorry I'm
late."

Dwight greeted his son with a manly handshake
and embrace. He used that as a time to whisper in his
ears, "Don't forget what I told you last night.
Behave the way I expect you to. And apologize to
Dawn."

"Enough already," said Rachelle. "Can I get a
hello as well?"

Raheem and Rachelle looked in each other's
eyes. He knew she knew and that's all that really
mattered between the two. For all their lives they
never had to apologize to each other verbally. The
unspoken words were felt from the looks they gave
each other. She would talk to him later. He was
changing and she didn't quite recognize the man he
was becoming; seems like she wasn't the only one
holding back their manifestation from child to
adulthood.

He made the rounds to everyone in the house and
addressed Leigh last. He pulled her into his arms,
holding her longer than he had held anyone else. He
inhaled the sweet smell of her perfume, closing his
eyes and savoring the way she made him feel.

"Hey there, beautiful, I've missed you," he whispered into her ear.

She blushed as she placed a quick kiss on his lips. "You saw me last night, silly." She chuckled innocently.

As they were coming out of their embrace, Dawn and Kenyon walked through the partially closed door. Dwight saw the look in Dawn's eyes. He felt bad for her, but she had to understand that Raheem was not the man for her. Truthfully, he didn't feel that he was the right man for Leigh as well. Raheem was heading down a path that none of them had seen coming, and he didn't want anyone to be victim to whatever lay ahead.

"Happy Thanksgiving, Dawn," said Dwight, pulling her into his arms. Turning his attention to Kenyon, Dwight gave him a manly hug and said, "Happy Thanksgiving, Kenyon."

"Happy Thanksgiving, everyone," said Dawn. She pulled her eyes away from Raheem and Leigh, spying Rachelle and Zion whispering to each other. She hoped that her friend wasn't divulging what they spoke about last night to her newfound love.

Rachelle and Dawn met halfway.

"How are you doing today?" asked Rachelle.

Dawn nodded in an attempt to reassure Rachelle with her answer. "Good. I'm fine." In a way the gesture was her way of reassuring herself as well as those around looking at her.

She had stood in the mirror most of the morning giving herself a much-needed pep talk. She had prayed to God for Him to send her the type of man that would be the perfect husband for her. A man that would love her for her and she could love him for him. Her talk to herself was to let God do what he needed to do and she needed to accept the fact that Raheem was not and would not be the man for her.

After saying hello to Kenyon, Rachelle instructed everyone to go into the dining room. Leigh had done such a beautiful job setting the table. She had arranged the napkins into little swans, placing them in the center of the plates. The cornucopia was in the center, but Rachelle knew they wouldn't last for long. She needed the room to place the turkey and all the trimmings she had prepared earlier.

"I would like to thank Leigh for coming over early and offering her help to finish up the desserts and setting this table in such a beautiful way," said

Rachelle offering Leigh a genuine smile. "I'm thankful that I have each and every one of you in my life and I wouldn't want it any other way."

Rachelle nodded in the direction of her father; it was her signal to him to take over the welcomes and the traditions that they were accustomed to on Thanksgiving Day.

"If Lily were alive today, she would be beaming from the love and friendship in this room. I know that she is looking down on us all from heaven," he said while looking up. "We are grateful that each of you could make it here to celebrate another day of thanks and gratitude for the things and people God has placed in our lives. Before the prayer that Pastor Brown will deliver, we will go around the room and everyone will say a quick thank you for one thing or more if you feel very grateful." Dwight sat turned to his right and gave the floor to Raheem.

Standing, Raheem looked at each person trying to figure out what is it really had to be thankful for. He had already thanked God for the business Kenyon and him had and how well it was doing. So it didn't seem right for him to be thankful for that again. It wasn't his place to announce how thankful he was that his sister had finally claimed the love that she obviously deserved after all these years. He was thankful for his father's good health even if they didn't see eye to eye at times lately.

What did he really have to be thankful for?

"I have so many things I have said thank you Lord for already time and time again," he said. "I'm not quite sure what I want to mention today. I guess I'm just thankful for this time that I have to spend with each of you."

Dwight looked at him with a furrowed brow. That was all he had to offer. He really didn't know this person sitting at his table anymore.

"Leigh, the floor is yours," said Dwight, still reveling in the easy way out of saying something they didn't already know and hear.

Leigh stood on shaking legs. She wasn't used to all eyes being on her. She didn't know what to say because she had never been a part of anything like this before. Listening to Raheem, she didn't want to say the same thing even though that is how she felt as well.

"Um, I would like to say thank you to Dwight and Rachelle for opening their home to me, allowing me to experience a real Thanksgiving." She stopped to think a little bit more. She saw Dwight and Rachelle smiling at her. It seemed they were always smiling at her, something she would have to get used to. "I am most grateful for having my eyes open to see what being a part of a close knit bunch of people really means and feels like."

"We're glad to have you," said Dwight. "Zinnia, please."

Zinnia stood and said, "Like you Leigh I am grateful for everyone in this room. You know being the First Lady of a church every member is a member of our family. Though not all of them willingly open their home to us we are thankful that we can open our home and hearts to them. I am most thankful that God has been using me as a vessel to get his message to many."

"I couldn't agree with you more, honey," said Pastor Brown. "We never know when we will get a call saying our prayers are needed to help heal a sick, take away a worry, or in whatever way we are needed. But we are thankful that we are needed and our work is touching many. I am thankful for every day we are alive and healthy so we can continue the work that

God has set before us. I'm fighting the urge to preach, so I'm going to sit down."

They all laughed.

"Well I guess it's my turn," said Rachelle standing up. "I thankful for being able to come out from under the dark cloud I have been living in for the past fifteen years. And although every day will not be easy, I am grateful that I have the memory of my mother and I can still feel her love in my heart. I know many people have suffered a lost like me and I am not alone." Again she turned and looked at Leigh. "The best part is knowing that I have each of you to help me make the necessary changes within myself to move on and be really happy."

A thought popped into Rachelle's mind as she was reclaiming her seat. *Create a way for those like you who are suffering as you have to know they are not alone.* She nodded to herself in agreement with her new goal to be a servant to God's work.

Zion took the floor next. "These are some of the best days, when we can spend time with friends and family and just bask in their presence. I wouldn't have it any other way. I am thankful for finally being able to express my undying love to

Rachelle after all these years of keeping it to myself in fear of rejection. I'm grateful that she has reciprocated my feelings, and what I believe to be God's blessing putting us together to one day be a family and continue to work in his name."

Those words were unexpected to Rachelle's ears and heart. She blushed and smiled, tears pooling in her eyes. This truly was a happy day for her. Nothing or no one could take the joy out of her heart. She reached for Zion's hand and squeezed it.

"Is there really anything left to be said?" asked Kenyon. All eyes were now on him as he stood tall with pride exuding from his body. "I look forward to these kinds of get together. Not only for the food." They laughed. "But also for the company of some interesting people that God has placed into my life. You know I lost my parents before I got a chance to even know them, but I have all of you for so long that I never really felt as though I was missing anything.

"You cannot miss what you don't know in the first place, right?" He paused looking around to see if they were all in agreement. They were all nodding. "I'm thankful for the business Raheem and I have.

It's doing wonderfully. I'm grateful for everyone's happiness in this room. Whenever one hurts, I hurt, and I can truly say we are all happy on this day."

Standing Dawn straightened her clothes, "Last but not least, right?" she said. "I'm thankful for new beginnings and clearer vision. I am thankful for the things to come."

"Let us all stand and join hands," said Pastor Brown. "Bow your heads, close your eyes, but open your heart to the love of the Lord. I promise not to be long. Lord, as we congregate before you, we say thank you for your grace and mercy.

"We thank you for the ones who prepared the meals and pray for those who didn't have a morsel to eat today. We thank you for providing us each other to keep us from being alone and pray for those who are lonely. Lord, we ask you to bless the food and allow it to provide nourishment in our bodies. Keep us safely together in your loving son's name, Amen."

"Amen," they all said.

"Let's eat," said Kenyon. They all laughed at him again, for only he would scream that out.

"Ok, well Kenyon let's put the turkey on the side board if you don't mind giving me a hand," said

Rachelle. "Zion, Raheem, you can help place the side dishes in the center of the table while Daddy craves the turkey."

"Do you need any other help?" asked Leigh.

"No, I don't. Plus you've helped me enough today."

Dawn looked at Leigh with a partial scowl. This was not the day or time to be jealous, but she felt as though Leigh was trying to take her place. First, she took Raheem from her, and now she was stealing Rachelle's attention as well. She went into the kitchen to help bring out the food without bothering to ask if she was needed. That's the way to help; you just do it. *You don't have to ask*, she thought.

"Dawn, are you alright?" asked Kenyon.

"Of course I am. This is a great day. Why wouldn't I be alright?"

"I was only asking. Never mind what I said."

Only thing left to be brought in was the gravy boat. Dawn felt really silly walking into the dining room with such a tiny thing. Now she wished she had just sat in her chair like everyone else waiting for the food to make its way around the table and digging in. As she made her way back to the table she wanted to have a reason to walk pass Leigh so she could accidentally spill some of the gravy on to her white shirt, but they sat on different sides of the table, so she wouldn't be able to justify her actions. She said a quick prayer, *Lord, please help me to get rid of these hateful feelings. I know Leigh is not my problem with Raheem. Please continue to work on me.*

* * *

They ate and enjoyed each other's company. The conversation was nothing serious, even Leigh had finally loosened up and was having a really good time with everyone. She had been invited by everyone at the table except for Dawn to attend church on Sunday. She told them she would think about it, but she already felt as though she would go just to see what was God really about. She didn't feel pressured or judged because she didn't have a relationship with God. While she enjoyed the savory candied yams, she wondered if there was a God, and if there were a God, what was it he was trying to tell her.

Chapter Twenty-Seven

"Dinner was wonderful," said Zion as he and Rachelle stood outside on the back deck, alone for the first time all day.

"I had a great time also. It was really nice to have everyone around us and feeling joyous and blessed." He moved closer to her and waited for a comment. When she said nothing, he added "I'll take those instead of the tension we've been feeling lately whenever Raheem has been in the room."

She stared out into the distance as he held her tightly from behind. She had her arms crossed over his. Rachelle drank up the love she was feeling all day and at this very moment. "I don't want to speak about him right now. Let's talk about us."

"I like that topic," he said, kissing her on the nose. "What about us? I think we've been doing really well so far."

"We have, but you said something today that we really never spoke about. I want to know if that's the way you really feel."

Zion tilted her head up with his fingers, looking straight into her beautiful brown eyes. Placing a tender kiss on her lips, he said,

"Rachelle, nothing would make me happier than to marry you today and start our family. But I don't want to scare you. Those words I said in front of our friends and family is what I feel deep down in my heart."

Her eyes danced with joy. She never thought the day would come when she could feel this type of love from someone other than her parents. It seemed as though her life ended the day her mother died. While she aged, she stopped living, and she needed to make a promise to herself that no matter what happened, she would to take the good with the bad and most of all continue to be a part of the living. She almost missed out on the man she had loved all of her life because of her lifelong mourning.

"What would you do if I said I was ready for you to ask me? I don't want to waste another day of my life being afraid." She waited for him to respond. She could see his eyes shifting back and forth, contemplating. Slowly, she could see the corners of his mouth turning upwards in a Cheshire cat smile.

"Well, then I should schedule a talk with your father. I need to ask for his blessing before I can get down on one knee and propose. I want to do everything right."

"Don't take too long," she said, kissing him again, this time a little deeper.

Breaking from their embrace, Zion led Rachelle back inside. "I'm ready for some more dessert."

She rubbed his stomach in a playful manner. "You better watch out. You may put on a few pounds before you get into that tux."

"Never that, but I do need to try every dessert, even if it's a little bit."

Having heard a bit of their conversation, Dwight headed in their direction and asked, "What's the occasion?" He looked from Zion to Rachelle.

"Oh, Daddy, there's no occasion," Rachelle said, trying to get past him. But he blocked their way.

"I know I heard something about a tux. Why do you need a tux? I haven't heard about any functions coming up." Dwight tried to hold back his smile.

"Mr. D., we're going to have to schedule a time when you're not too busy for us to have a heart to heart, man to man."

Dwight allowed Rachelle to pass, but blocked Zion's way. "No better time than the present." Placing one hand on his back and pointing with the other, Dwight led Zion back out onto the deck.

Turning back to look over his shoulder, Zion saw Rachelle watching her him. She didn't seem nervous or afraid for him, but delighted. He drew from her the positive spirit and courage to do what needed to be done in order to fulfill not only his dreams but Rachelle's as well. Who would have thought that him making that one statement today would lead him to this very conversation he was about to have with Mr. D. He surely didn't wake up with this in his mind, but it was in his heart, always has been.

"Let's have a seat, young man. All that food is taking its toll on an old man such as me."

"Mr. D., I could only hope to be in such a good shape when I'm your age."

He waved off Zion's kind words. Dwight knew that if Lily were alive she would be fussing at him about the things he ate and his non-existing exercise regimen. She would make him eat better and be more conscious about his health. Without her, life had been life, but not the life he would have had if she were still alive. He knew how Rachelle felt. He missed Lily just as much, if not more. Since she'd died he had never contemplated being with anyone else, partly in fear of hurting Rachelle anymore than she was already hurting. And also because he wasn't sure he could love anyone else the way he loved Lily. He didn't want to experience that kind of loss ever again. His heart couldn't take it.

"What do you want to talk to me about?"

Zion shifted in his seat a little. He unbuttoned the top button of his shirt; he had the courage before, but all of a sudden he felt like something was gripping his throat. He tried clearing it but the tightness stayed the same.

Witnessing how uncomfortable he was, Dwight said, "You know we've known each other for quite some time. I remember you coming over and pounding that basketball out there with the twins. We're like family. As a matter of fact, you are a part of this family. You have been for a very long time." He leaned forward. "Don't be afraid of showing me your feelings."

"Mr. D.," Zion began, more assured, "I've waited for Rachelle for most of my life. I had to be certain she was ready to move past the pain she had been feeling for all these years. When I returned from school and she was still struggling, I almost gave up hope."

Standing he looked out into the vastness of the yard. He pictured a beautiful spring day and a makeshift altar where he waited as Rachelle made her way down an aisle created by their friends and family who reveled in their love for one another and her beauty.

"I love Rachelle very much. And nothing would make me happier than to make her my wife. But I cannot ask her until you give me the permission and your blessings. Without those two things, I will have no need for a tuxedo." Turning around he faced Dwight.

Dwight was already nodding as he stood and shook Zion's hand. "Of course you have my blessing. Man, it's about time."

Zion couldn't help but smile. He was finally in a place where his purpose in life was starting to go in the right direction. He knew with Rachelle by his side the things they would do together would be endless. She had a heart of pure gold and she would be a wonderful wife and mother. He couldn't wait to go out tomorrow and purchase a ring and properly ask Rachelle to marry him.

"Thanks, Mr. D. I won't let you down."

"Son, I know you won't. Zinnia and Zachary have done a wonderful job raising you. When will you be finishing school?"

"I'm actually done. I don't think being a preacher is for me. Since I minored in psychology as well, I'm considering working in a field where I can help my people without being scrutinized."

"I understand. Well either way, your parents raised you right and I'm not worried. I believe in you."

"Thank you. That makes me feel really good."

Together the two men made their way back inside. Rachelle and Dawn were in the kitchen packing up take home boxes for each person. Leigh and Zinnia were at the sink, one washing while the other dried.

Rachelle stopped what she was doing when she heard the door open. She looked at her father and could see no sign of what he said to Zion on his face. Zion's face was masked as well. She didn't want to ask in front of the others what was said, so she decided to wait until she could get one of them alone to find out.

"Mom, whenever you're ready to go I am, too," Zion said.

"We're just about done here, love. I know your father is asleep in the den, so if you don't mind waking him I will be ready in a few."

Zion went to do as he was asked, leaving Rachelle wondering.

Placing two different containers into each bag, Rachelle and Dawn brought the bags into the dining room, resting them on the table. The guys were stretching, trying to shake off the feeling of tiredness that followed after such a luscious meal. It was a great time had by all, but now they were all ready to go to sleep.

"Once again I want to thank you all for sharing this day with us and I hope we are blessed with another day where we can do this again. Get home safely," said Dwight.

He beamed with pride that everything happened without any incident. Rachelle and Raheem didn't have any words. But he also noticed that Raheem didn't say anything to Dawn as he had told him to do. He needed to apologize to that young lady.

He pulled Raheem into to the kitchen quickly, getting up in his face so only he could hear his words. "I don't know if you were too drunk last night to remember what I told you, but I will remind you. Dawn has been around most of your life, and you need to apologize to her. If you're not interested in her, that's fine, but you still need to respect her, so apologize now before she leaves."

Raheem made no movement. The pair watched as Dawn headed for the door. She turned and waved at Dwight.

"Right now, Raheem. Do I make myself clear?" he said through clenched teeth.

Dwight made him feel like a teenager again. His tone and look reminded him of the time he had yelled at the teacher who accused him of cheating on a test. Dwight scolded him for being rude to the teacher even though he didn't do what he was accused of. Dwight forced him to make a public apology.

"Yes, sir," Raheem finally said, lowering his gaze to the floor.

"Well get to it then."

Dwight walked away from him and over to Dawn to give her a fatherly hug. "I will see you Sunday at church. Before I forget to tell you, I love your hair."

Smiling, Dawn said, "Thank you."

"Hey, Dawn, can I speak to you for a second?"

She looked at Raheem with trepidation. What else could he possibly have left to say to her after last night? She didn't want to be embarrassed in front of everyone. She already felt like a fool and purposely stayed away from him all evening.

"I'm a bit tired and Kenyon's ready to go, so can it wait?"

Raheem was about to say yes when he felt a firm hand on his shoulder. He knew without looking over his shoulder that it was his father. "It won't take long, I promise. Or I can drive you home if you would like. Either way I need to speak to you today."

Feeling a little uneasy, Dawn thought quickly about what she should do. She had made it through the dinner without any incidents, and she really wanted to end it on a positive note without any drama. At the same time she really wanted to hear what Raheem had to say to her that couldn't wait. Turning to

Kenyon, she looked at him to see if he knew what was going on, but he shrugged and shook his head.

"I guess you can give me a lift home."

"Alright, then everyone once again it was lovely," Raheem said, leading Dawn out the door. Before he got all the way outside, he turned back and kissed Leigh on the cheek and told her to meet him back at his place.

Everyone followed them out, and Rachelle made an attempt to grab Zion before he got too far out the door behind them, but he was determined to leave as well. He didn't want to give her any idea of what her father's response was to his request. "I got to go, honey. My parents are tired."

"Well how did it go with my Dad?" she asked, concerned.

"I can't talk about that right now. I will tell you later." He kissed her lips and walked out. She stood at the door, watching him walk away. She couldn't help but wonder what her future held.

Chapter Twenty-Eight

Dawn sat in Raheem's SUV, the seatbelt tight against her, making her feel as though she was strapped to the electric chair. She was very uncomfortable being in a closed off surrounding where she couldn't easily get up and leave if she needed or wanted to.

Other than the turn signal indicator, the vehicle was in complete silence for the first few miles. The uncomfortable silence was beginning to drive Dawn crazy. Her legs were now shaking while she twirled one of her locs around her finger.

Raheem looked at her from the corner of his eyes and chuckled.

"What's so funny?" she asked.

"You are. We have known each other for a long time. I'd like to believe that we have been good friends for all those years."

She didn't look in his direction, but she did nod in agreement. "We were."

His brow furrowed. "Were? So you mean we're not friends anymore?"

"Look, Raheem, I don't see how we can still be friends after what has happened between us."

"I don't understand," he said, confusion filling his eyes. "I was drunk and I said a few things that may not have been nice or what I really meant, but I do value your friendship."

"It's not only what you said that's the problem," she said. Her heart was pounding. She was having a difficult time formulating the proper words to describe how she was feeling…how he had made her feel when the words of hate spewed from his lips. His words danced in her mind - *The only way I would touch you again would be if I had a few drinks in me. Maybe even something stronger.* His final comment seared into the back of her mind as if he had branded the words there with a hot iron rod - *You'll never be as good as Leigh is, no matter what God you serve.* Those words were not from someone who cared about her. Those words were not induced by alcohol; she thought they were. She had heard someplace that what you say while under the influence of drugs or alcohol is how you really feel. Those substances relaxed you enough to speak your mind. She didn't know how true it was, but right now that's not what she wanted to believe.

"Hey, Dawn, are you still with me?" he asked now parked in front her apartment complex. He had parked the car and watched her for a little while before he'd called her name. He could see she was in deep thought and confusion was written all over her face. It looked painful to him.

Continuing to look straight ahead, not wanting him to see the pain in her eyes, she said, "Yes, I'm here. I'm just thinking."

"What's on your mind? You know one minute you were saying it wasn't just my words, and then the next you're very quiet and not saying anything to me." Unfastening his seatbelt, Raheem lifted Dawn's chin toward him so that they were eye-to-eye. His father always told him it was rude to not look into someone's eyes as you spoke. "Why don't you tell me what's on your mind. I'm sober today."

He chuckled.

But she didn't. Dawn's lack of laughter prompted him to sit up straight.

She looked at all his features; from the stubble on his normally clean-shaven baldhead to his slightly moisten succulent lips. She looked into his eyes and said, "Raheem, to me we made love. To you we had a not so memorable moment. I wanted more from you than just…friendship. I have friends, but I want a man who loves me for me and wants to hold me and love me every day for the rest of my life."

He cleared his throat. "You know at first I was only apologizing to make my father happy."

Her head whipped around as she reached for the door handle. "You're only here because of Mr. D? Wow, see this is why I didn't want to be bothered with hearing you out. Somehow it always comes back to bite me on the—never mind it doesn't even matter."

Opening the door, she jumped from SUV. She was digging in her purse trying to find her keys.

Trying to catch her before she had gotten too far, Raheem almost left the truck running. After tuning the engine off, he ran after her.

"Can you please just wait a minute?" he asked, out of breath.

"For what, so you can insult me some more? Go home, Raheem! Leave me alone. I get it, ok." She was trying once again to hold it together in his presence. She didn't want him to see her cry. She had already given him her most prized position and she couldn't get that back now, and he didn't really want it in the first place. So she had nothing more to offer him or give him.

"So you're not going to hear me out?"

Stopping in her tracks, she spun around to face him. He hadn't expected her to stop short, which took him off guard and he almost ran right into her.

"You have a minute to say what you need to say and then I'm gone, so use your time wisely."

Raheem had seen Dawn upset, but not as mad as she was at that moment. The brisk Georgia night was not the reason he suddenly felt a chill. Hey eyes were like daggers and the defensive way she had her arms crossed over chest told him she meant what she said.

"Seriously, I was telling the truth in the car, but now that I'm here and I see how much you're hurting I really do feel bad," he said watching her tap her booted foot on the concrete. "I don't know how my father found out, nor do I care, but I do know it was a good thing he did coming and confronting me. I didn't mean anything that I said."

"Oh really so I can add up to the likes of Leigh now? You can willingly be with me without being inebriated?"

Raheem sighed. This was more difficult than he thought it would be. The things he needed to say he wasn't saying and the things he didn't want to say or mean kept coming out.

"Look, I love you, but like a sister. I can't give you anything else other than that. I just don't see you in that manner. I'm sorry."

"You're sorry, I get it. I'm sorry also."

He looked confused. "What do you have to be sorry for?"

"For not being the right shade or the perfect woman that you could ever find attractive enough to be interested in. Most of all I'm sorry for giving you my virginity when you didn't deserve it. I wish I could take it back, but I can't."

He didn't know what else to say to her. He waited for her to say more, but his minute was up. She walked away leaving him with his guilty conscious.

* * *

Slamming the door behind her, Dawn entered the apartment. Kenyon was sitting on the couch. "What's the matter?" he asked, concern in his voice.

She was fighting with her boots as she tried yanking them off. "Raheem is my problem."

"What happened now?" Kenyon moved over to where she was standing still fighting with her shoes. Pushing her hand away, he placed one hand on the heel and the other in the front, slipping the boots from her feet. "I know you're upset, but you can't be angry with your shoes or the poor door you slammed when you came in."

"Sorry, but I'm so angry." Her top lip quivered.

"Come on over here and sit down and tell me what happened." Kenyon pointed her toward the couch. "Do you want some water or juice?"

Shaking her head, she took several deep breaths. She had prayed to God for healing and guidance, but here she was once again feeling pain. "Am I really that hard to love?"

"Of course not. We all love you, you know that, right?"

"Then why is it that Raheem won't love me back? What does he see in Leigh that I don't have?" She couldn't contain the tears anymore. They made their way down her cheeks two at a time.

"Sometimes you look for love in the wrong place. It may be the case with Raheem and you. You two aren't that different, but you're too blind to see that." Kenyon's mouth was becoming dry. He wished she had taken the drink he had offered her because right now he would be guzzling it down.

The tears were coming down faster than she could wipe them. "I don't understand. How could I be wrong? We all grew up together, we've been friends forever. Isn't that the best kind of relationship, the one that starts out as friends before lovers."

"Yes, it is. But, Dawn, you have other people around you that have been and still are loving you for you. Someone who takes notice in you and the things that you do and wants to one day be a part of it. But you have only taken interest in one man when there are others."

"Who, Kenyon...who could there possibly be?" Her voice went up a decibel. "I want to know who. Introduce him to me, please."

Pounding his fist on his chest, he said, "Me! Damn it, me."

Two lonely tears made their way down her face. Her mouth falling open, she mouthed the word *you.*

Chapter Twenty-Nine

"Yes, me." He looked at her with a cross between being surprised and being offended. "Is that so hard to believe?"

"You've never said anything. And I don't look like the kind of lady you usually entertain."

He chuckled at her audacity. Rolling his eyes, he allowed his head to tilt back, taking what seemed like a cleansing breath from the heavens. He chewed on his bottom lip while taking off his glasses and wiping away the perspiration he felt gathering on his face. He had let his secret out of the bag. And now it was too late to take it back.

"I would never date or entertain, as you put it, anyone that looks anything like you. You know why?" She shook her head from side to side. "I didn't want to always feel as though I was measuring these ladies up to you. They would always pale in comparison to you."

"Why didn't you ever say anything to me?"

"Dawn, I figured you would one day figure it out for yourself. I mean come on," he said standing and pacing the length between the couch and the coffee table. "When we realized Rachelle wouldn't get an apartment with you like we all thought she would, you know me with Raheem in our place, you ladies in yours, I decided I had to be there to keep you safe. That's why I agreed to move in with you. It didn't hurt that I got to see you every day."

She couldn't believe what her ears were delivering into the cerebral cortex of her mind. She was quickly looking for the visible signs through the years she had known Kenyon, and still she couldn't pinpoint anything that stood out. She was amazed.

"It's too late for us now," she said. "Even if I had known, it's simply too late now."

"Why is it too late?"

He sat on the coffee table looking her in her eyes, searching for the one glimmer of a chance for them to try and see where their relationship could go from here on out.

The words she said not only shocked him, but it did her as well. "After what happened between Raheem and me, you won't want anything to do with me in that manner ever again." She paused. "It would put a sour taste on your view of me."

Grabbing her hands between his two strong, well manicured hands, Kenyon said, "Why don't you give me a chance to make that decision for myself? We all have demons and skeletons hidden. Who are we to judge?"

"I don't know if you can take hearing it. It's even hard for me to believe it."

"Trust me, I promise I'm not like other men."

Dawn looked at Kenyon as if it were the first time she was really seeing him. He was a handsome man. He was not buff, but there was no place that her eyes could see where there was anything flabby. His brownish-green eyes were invigorating and his lips every time he licked them were inviting.

"Let's say I'm willing to give you a chance to show me that I am worth loving the way I desire to be love and I tell you my secret, how can you guarantee me that you won't have a change of heart? You would be kicking the stake that Raheem placed in my heart all the way through and I would be devastated."

"Give a chance," was all he said and all he was going to say. He had opened the door and it was up to her to walk in if she chose to.

She sat and thought for a few minutes more and she couldn't do it. Her heart was very vulnerable

right now and she couldn't deal with rejection as
yet.

"I'm sorry—"

He cut her off. "Before you say anything else,
let me say this. I will not approach you again. So
depending on what you were about to say if you turn
me down and then change your mind, you will have to
come to me. And it may be too late."

She wasn't expecting that either. But she had
to follow her first instinct and keep their
friendship as it had always been. "I'm sorry, Kenyon,
I just can't do this. Not now."

He swallowed the hard lump that was sitting in
his throat. One thing was for certain; he did not
regret letting her in on how he really felt about
her. "Fine, I respect your feelings and nothing has
to change."

He said the words, but was praying it was true,
for his sake. He had strong feelings for her and
watched for years as she pined over Raheem from a
distance. In his mind his cousin was stupid for not
wanting a woman as grand as Dawn.

Dawn picked up her boots and headed toward her
room, but not before saying, "I really am sorry. I

wish it was you I had in my eyes all these years. Maybe it will be one day."

He said nothing aloud, but he thought, *from your lips to God's ear, into my heart.*

* * *

Dawn stood with her back up against her closed bedroom door. She was still reveling at the confession from Kenyon. "Lord, is this how you planned it? Zion with Rachelle, Kenyon with me, and Raheem looking for love outside our tight inner circle?"

She felt her cell phone vibrating in her purse. When she retrieved it, the Caller ID showed a picture of Rachelle. She smiled, quickly answering.

"Hey, what's up?"

"Are you ok? What did Raheem want from you?" she asked.

She decided not to divulge her conversation with Kenyon even though she wanted to so much. For right now it was best if no one knew except for the two of them. "He wanted to apologize for insulting me the other night."

"Is that all?" Nodding as though they were sitting in front of each other, Dawn replied, "I'm positive." She paused, remembering something Raheem had said to her. "Hey did you tell Mr. D. about what happened?"

"No! Why do you ask?"

"Because the only reason he apologized was due to Mr. D. insisting that he do it, at least at first anyway."

They both sat saying nothing, each in her own world of unresolved thoughts. Each wanting to share with the other, but wanting to keep her thoughts to herself at the same time.

"I guess I better let you go. I wanted to check on you that's all. I love you, Dawn." Rachelle had felt the need to reassure her friend. Something about the way Dawn was acting all day made her feel the need to remind her that she always had a warm place in her heart, no matter what.

"I love you, too."

Chapter Thirty

Zinnia was sitting in the family room with her Bible open on her lap and her eyes closed. She was in deep thought after a long conversation with her eternal father. She had been praying for everyone that she had the opportunity to break bread with today and all the parishioners of the church. Zachary had already gone up to bed and now she was sitting and enjoying the silence surrounding her mind, body, and soul.

Zion walked in. He kept quiet as he watched her, trying to discern if she were asleep or thinking.

She spoke with her eyes still closed and head tilted back. "What is it you need, Zion?"

"I will never get used to you doing that," he said, walking over to have a seat next to her.

"One day when you're a parent you will understand." Patting him on the knee, she continued, "Did you need something? Or do you like watching me enjoy my clear mind?"

"Both I guess."

Adjusting her body, she gave him her full attention. "What's on your mind?"

His parents have always been very good at listening without a judgmental ear to everyone that came to them, even him and that was why their following was growing all the time. People liked the down to earth Pastor and First Lady of Abiding Faith Tabernacle.

"I need your help, Mom."

He was taking it slowly when it came to speaking his mind this evening. But the fatigue from the long day coupled with the enormous amount of food she felt compelled to consume made her want to tell him to spit it out already. But she kept her cool and let him go at his own pace.

She nodded.

"Mom, I need you to help me pick out the perfect engagement ring for Rachelle tomorrow."

If she were sleep before, his words would have been like a sobering cup of strong black coffee. "Is that what you and Dwight were speaking about?"

"Yes."

"Alright then, um I don't see why that will be a problem. After your Thanksgiving speech, we knew it was only a matter of time. But Zion," she paused, "make certain marrying Rachelle is what you really want. She's very vulnerable."

"Mother," he said, using the name he called her when he wanted to let her know he was being serious, "I have waited for Rachelle to come out from under her mourning fog for fifteen years. Do you really think I would take advantage of her in that way?"

"Honey, that's not what I said or meant," she said reassuringly. "I know you have loved her for a very long time. However, she is changing before our very eyes, every day and it seems like the healing that should have happened over the years is only now happening rapidly." Zinnia gave an innocent laugh. "She almost reminds me of a Bonsai. They do most of their growing underground for all those years, but once it's time to grow above the soil, it happens so quickly."

"I guess she's been healing on the inside for some time now. She just had to allow it to show on the outside. Is that what you're saying?"

"Exactly."

"So will you help me?"

Kissing him on the cheek, she replied, "Of course I will."

"Thanks, Mom." His cell phone rang the cute little jingle signifying a call that could only be from one person.

"Hello, Rachelle."

On the other end of the phone, Rachelle was lying across her bed on her stomach, bouncing her legs. She couldn't get her mind to rest; she really needed to know what had happened between Zion and her father. "What did you guys speak about?" she asked forgoing the regular greetings.

A smile turned his mouth, lighting up his face. "You're relentless, aren't you? Why don't you ask Mr. D.?" He really didn't want to give her too much information. In a way he wanted her to think that her father had not given his blessings in an attempt to surprise her when he proposed officially.

"Zion, can you please tell me?"

"Get some rest, Rachelle. I'll speak with you tomorrow. I'm not sure if I will have a chance to see you because I'm helping my mother with something."

Rachelle wasn't thrilled that she didn't get any closer to an answer. She wanted to pout, but the thought made her laugh.

"What's so funny?"

"Nothing. Goodnight."

Before Zion could say anything else, Rachelle disconnected the call. She couldn't believe that she was behaving like a lovesick teenager. She laughed at herself one more time before heading to the shower. She didn't experience this as a teen, but now in her thirties she was dealing with butterflies and giddiness.

Chapter Thirty-One

The days were moving fast to Dawn. The store has been so busy since Black Friday. Dawn got to work early every day and left late. She had received quite a few orders for her handcrafted jewelry, and was doing her best to make them at night. Due to her being so busy, she hadn't had a moment to even think about the way things had unfolded on Thanksgiving.

When she returned home from work, she was wound up tight. Her body was so tired she didn't want to do anything, but lie down right inside the doorway. She decided to at least make it over to where Kenyon sat on the couch.

"Hey, you look like you've been ran over by a steamroller."

She rolled her eyes, not being able to think of anything snappy to say back. "Ha ha funny."

Already heading into the kitchen, he asked, "Are you hungry? I made some spaghetti. I can fix you a plate if you want." He paused with the plate in his hand over the pot, waiting for her to answer.

Dawn didn't answer. She had tilted her head back on the couch as she slept. Replacing the lid on the pot, Kenyon took her in. She looked too peaceful for

him to wake up. He walked into her room, something he
didn't do often to retrieve the crocheted blanket
that she had made to throw over her.

His intentions were to cover her, put away the
food, and then call it a night himself, but looking
at her sleeping seemed more interesting to him than
doing anything else. Sitting in the chair, he watched
her until his eyes slowly closed, bringing into the
dream world.

A disoriented Dawn was the first to wake. She
didn't remember falling asleep. Making it safely home
was her main goal and she had done that; everything
else was not relevant to her. She took in the
crocheted blanket from the foot of her bed thrown
over her and Kenyon sitting in the chair across from
her; instantly, she thought about the talk they had
on Thanksgiving night.

His thoughts and caring words were really sweet
and a part of his natural character. She knew he
could've been saying whatever he thought would be
necessary to make her feel better after the way
Raheem had treated her. But she hadn't told him about
what had been going on between them; she hadn't even
divulged the information to Rachelle. Some things she

felt the need to keep to herself. She needed to know exactly how much of what's going on did Kenyon need to know, if anything at all.

How do I approach the subject without given him false hope? she thought.

* * *

Kenyon was stiff; it was the consequences from sleeping half the night on the chair. But it was busy at *Soft Hands* and he needed to put his kinks aside to take care of the needs of their clients.

His mind had been distracted by the things Dawn kept saying would change his mind about her. He couldn't see how anything would make him stop caring about her so deeply. He knew that she was still dealing with the rejection she felt from her parents even though she would never be one to say it to anyone.

Kenyon had made up his mind to find out the things that had been going on in order to move on without regrets. He wanted to make certain that his decision to not pursue Dawn was well thought out and justified. She could be his blessing and he didn't want to miss out.

He had left a note on Raheem's clipboard telling him that he wanted to have a quick talk with him later. This was the day when everything would come to light.

The day had been long and brutal. After finishing up with his last client, Kenyon went into the yoga room to stretch out the stiffness he'd been feeling all day. In the lotus position, a very focused Kenyon hadn't noticed Raheem entering the studio. They both had always taken pride in their bodies and mental health.

"Hey, man, I hardly saw you all day," Raheem said. Grabbing a mat, he aligned it with the front of Kenyon's. He forwent the normal warm up and went straight into warrior pose.

Kenyon stood and joined him in the pose, being his mirror image. Even though they wouldn't be able to speak eye to eye, they would be face to face. While doing yoga was a way to meditate and relax, it was another way to see the truest of emotions on the other's face because yoga required a great deal of concentration and neither would be able to focus that hard on hiding the way they were truly feeling.

Kenyon watched Raheem closely, trying to play it cool on the way he approached the subject of Dawn. "You're really concentrating today, huh? Is something wrong with the books?"

"Nah, it's nothing to do with the business. It's personal."

Changing to warrior two, they both adjusted their footing. "So, what's up?"

"What's going on with you and Dawn and Leigh?"

Raheem lost his footing a little. He had almost lowered his arms when he heard Dawn's name mentioned in the same sentence as Leigh. "Leigh and I are dating, but as for Dawn, well there isn't anything up with us. We're friends, but not as close as we used to be because of some hurt feelings."

"Who did the hurting?"

"Well, I think—"

Kenyon cut him off. "No, not what you think, what is the truth." Kenyon was not doing anything anymore except for staring at Raheem. He concentrated on any facial movements that might indicate that his friend was lying to him.

"Dude, you know how Dawn has been after me for years, and she doesn't want to take no for an answer.

So you know one night I told her there's no way it will ever happen."

Something was off; that couldn't have been the only thing that was wrong between him and Dawn. That couldn't be the reason why he was standing on the sideline looking in because he never did make it known how he felt. "What else happened?"

"That's it." Raheem shrugged. "What more could there be other than her feelings got hurt?"

"She said something happened between you two. Something she thought would make me look at her in a different light." Kenyon's eyes narrowed and his jaw muscles flexed. He was gritting his teeth, holding back the thoughts that were swimming around in his head.

"Why don't you ask her if you want to know so badly?"

They had never fought about a female ever, but Raheem's defense was going up and Kenyon didn't believe a word he was saying. "You're my friend, man, and I have to live with her. So whatever you did affects my happy home."

"I don't have anything else to say on the subject of Dawn. You ask her and see what she says."

Raheem picked up his mat and placed it back where he had gotten it.

Kenyon couldn't understand; if nothing really happened, then why was Raheem getting so upset. If nothing happened between them other than the exchange of words, then there should be no reason for him to be ticked off. He watched him leave the studio, but he wasn't letting it go that easy.

Chapter Thirty-Two

Leigh and Rachelle had plans to have lunch across from the church at Panera's. Rachelle was finishing up a phone call and grabbing her purse to run across the street to meet Leigh when Ms. Zinnia walked in.

"Rachelle, we haven't had a session in awhile," Zinnia said. "Why don't we have one today? Now, if you don't already have lunch plans."

"I was about to go across to," she pointed in the direction of restaurant, "meet Leigh for a quick bite."

Zinnia turned and made an about face. "Can I join you ladies?"

"Sure."

Leigh was walking from the rear of the building as Zinnia and Rachelle made it across the street. She was wearing a boot cut pair of blue jeans, and a shear white top with a black lacy camisole underneath. Her hair was without the gel or mousse today; the natural curls were soft and bouncy all over her head. Rachelle had never seen her like this. Yes, she was still dressed sexily, but the change in her hair made her look different.

"I hope you weren't waiting for us long," said Rachelle, holding the door open for the others.

"No, I just got here. Hi, Ms. Zinnia."

Ms. Zinnia gave her the customary motherly hug she gave to everyone. "How are you, dear? I hope you don't mind me inviting myself to join you ladies."

"Not at all."

They all went to the counter and stared at the menu, each ordering soup and a sandwich. No one said anything until they were seated with the food. Ms. Zinnia did a quick blessing over the food before they dug in. Rachelle wasn't quite sure why Ms. Zinnia had wanted to eat with them, and Leigh wasn't sure what Rachelle had wanted.

"Leigh, you hair is beautiful," said Rachelle. "I didn't realize it was so soft and pretty."

She subconsciously reached for a fluff of loose curls. "Thank you."

"I know you ladies are wondering why I have invited myself here today," Ms. Zinnia said before taking a sip of her drink to clear her mouth of the roasted peppers and avocado sandwich. "Leigh, I wanted to offer you a chance to sit with me or Pastor Brown and talk about healing your heart. I know that you don't understand how someone you can't see can help you to heal."

"Look at me," Rachelle said, touching Leigh with one hand and her chest with the other. "I'm proof that you can heal if you give God a chance."

"I'm willing to come and talk to you, not your husband. He frightens me, but under one condition."

Zinnia wiped her mouth with a napkin, clasped her hand in front of her on the table, and gave Leigh her undivided attention. "Why is that?" she asked. Leigh was the first person to ever tell her that Zachary frightened her.

Leigh shrugged. "It's nothing that he's done or said, but he's a big man with a powerful voice. I wouldn't want to make him angry with my views and not believing that there's a God."

Zinnia and Rachelle laughed.

"Honey, Zachary is not like that at all," Zinnia said. "He's very caring and passionate. And no matter what you believe about God, he would never treat you any different than he does now. Do you understand?"

"Yes."

"Now what's that one condition?"

"I feel kind of silly saying it after what you said, but I still want you to know where I stand from day one."

Zinnia nodded and stretched her hand palm up waiting for her conditions.

"You don't try you force religion on me," Leigh said. "You will only help me to not feel lost anymore."

"That's not the way we work. We can show you scriptures and examples, but it's up to you to decide."

Keeping her tone softer than it was moments ago, Leigh agreed to meet with Ms. Zinnia.

* * *

Lunch turned out to be good. Leigh returned to her car heading to her next destination, and Rachelle and Zinnia returned back to the church. Rachelle had agreed to meet with Zinnia when she was done doing her work. Aside from doing work for the church, she had been using some of her time to research what it would take to start a program where people who were dealing with some sort of grief could come and meet with likeminded individuals. She would invite others who had been there and overcame the pain or obstacle

in their way, holding them stagnant in the past. She
didn't want others to take fifteen years or more to
move on.

Rachelle really wanted to involve Raheem in her
plans, but currently he wasn't acting like someone
who had dealt with his pain. For the first time ever
she realized while she had been taking care of her
brother and father, she may have been holding them in
the past with her and it wasn't fair to them to have
done that. Now that she had overcome and was moving
on, she didn't know if they could say the same.

I've been selfish, she thought. *Mother, please
help. I know you're up there watching over us and
shaking your head. I'm sorry. I should have done
better in your name. I'll fix it. I promise.*

Everything she found she printed even if she
didn't know if it would be helpful. She wanted it to
be a not for profit organization. Maybe Zion could
give talks along with her. After all they were a
couple now and would make a great team. She felt warm
and tingly inside just thinking of spend every waking
moment with him while helping others.

Chapter Thirty-Three

Raheem had tried to act like the things that happened between him and Dawn didn't matter, but for some reason, she was on his mind a lot now. He tried to drink it away because he didn't want to feel bad for allowing what occurred to happen. He felt bad about her and how he spoke to Kenyon.

He knew Kenyon was only asking because he cared about Dawn. He was the one who volunteered to be there for her in that apartment when no one else wanted to. At the time he thought that he was being noble, but now he realized it was more than what he thought. He recalled the stance Kenyon had as he asked him about what took place between Dawn and he.

Sitting in his apartment alone, waiting on Leigh to come over, Raheem decided he would call Kenyon and Dawn. He wanted to ask them to come over so that he could come clean with his friend and apologize the proper way to Dawn without being forced to do so. He felt as though she didn't quite believe or accept his last attempt at an apology. And in all fairness, she was right to feel that way. His apology was insincere; it was a command given by a father to a child and he had complied. Not this time.

He took a swallow from the bottle of beer he was
sucking down as he waited for someone to answer on
the other end of the phone. He would have driven to
them his self; however, he was on his fifth beer. He
was at least smart enough to know driving could be
very dangerous.

"Hello."

"Kenyon, that you?"

"Of course it's me. What's up, man?" he asked
him, annoyed.

"Is Dawn there? I wanted to know if you guys
would come over. I need to talk to you both."

He heard a rustling as though Kenyon had put
something over the mouthpiece of the phone. He
patiently waited for a response. He didn't want to
say anything else that could be construed as any ill-
natured words.

The rustling happened again. "I checked with
Dawn and she agreed. We'll be there in fifteen
minutes."

"Thanks, man."

No questions asked nor a goodbye, just an
agreement and then a disconnection. The effects of
the beer on him began to relax him more and more, but

he knew he needed to stay awake. To keep from dozing off, he got up and tried to straighten up a little. He hadn't been keeping his apartment as spotless as he normally would. He knew something was going on within himself, but he wasn't sure what it was. Since he didn't know, he couldn't get help or fix it. But he didn't want to bring others into the madness with him.

Leigh was the only one who connected with him. He believed that she too had been in the same darkness that was all consuming.

The knock on the door slightly sobered him. He had tried to think of the exact words he wanted to say to them, but nothing had come to mind. He did something he hadn't done in a while as he walked over to the door. He said a quick prayer. *Lord, I open my mouth tonight and I need you to help me make things right. Let me take ownership in whatever it was that I have done to hurt those who love and care for me.*

"Come on in," he said as he held the door open for Kenyon and Dawn. He pushed the door, allowing it to close softly. "Can I get either of you anything to drink?"

Dawn hadn't taken a seat; the trepidation on her face could be seen by them both. Kenyon rubbed her back, reinforcing what he had told her in the car on their way over. *"I'm there for you. If you want to leave, say the word and we are out of there."*

He led her to the couch and sitting right next to her, held her hands. "What did you want to talk to us about?"

Raheem retrieved a glass of water from the kitchen. He really wanted something stronger, but he didn't want to drink in front of them, giving them something else to judge him by.

"You know when you asked what had happened between Dawn and me, I was nonchalant about it. And I know I shouldn't have been that way."

Dawn looked at Kenyon, surprisingly. He hadn't mentioned that he went to Raheem questioning him about what had happened. She turned her attention back to Raheem.

Scooting forward on his seat, Raheem continued, "I'm ready to answer you now, but first," he turned looking directly at Dawn. He looked into her eyes and spoke as though they were the only ones in the room. "I need to say sorry to you. I'm sorry I wasn't able to prevent what had happened between us, but as you know I was drunk."

She held up her hands, trying to get him to stop talking. She didn't want Kenyon to hear about the night she now knows full heartedly was nothing but a big mistake. She thought giving herself to him in some way would have connected them to each other, but it didn't. She didn't want a man like him, who didn't seem to care about much these days. Without a doubt, Dawn didn't want him tarnishing Kenyon's views of her.

But Raheem ignored her protest and kept talking. "I'm sorry, Dawn. I really am. You have to believe I would never have willingly taken your virginity, then turn around, and try you the way that I did, if I were sober."

Dawn couldn't look in Kenyon's direction. His grip on her hand loosened. She could feel his eyes on her face. All she knew to do was to hang her head. She didn't want to see the shock or whatever other emotion she would see if she looked at him.

A sober Raheem would have noticed the defeated look on Dawn's face. However, the alcohol coursing through his body had loosened his tongue up and he wasn't done speaking yet.

His next comment was geared toward Kenyon. "You know I've never been one to kiss and tell. In this case, I'm going to tell you I had intimate relations with Dawn, but I don't remember it. That morning when I awoke to a body in my bed, I thought I had let my urges get the best of me and had slept with Leigh. But when I turned my head, there was—"

"There was who, Raheem?" asked Leigh. No one had heard when she had come in. She was so used to coming over and letting herself into the apartment because he usually left the door unlocked for her.

"It's not what you think," he said, getting up and running over to where Leigh was standing at the door. "I can explain."

"Who did you find in your bed?"

"Please come and sit down. We can all talk about this together," he said to her, trying to get her to move from where she was standing, but she would not budge.

Everything about her - the hand on the doorknob, the other on her hip, her eyes like daggers, and lips pursed – told him she was not going to be coerced to move inward.

Now feeling bad about the whole situation, Dawn said, "I'm to blame for this. Not Raheem."

"So it was you?" Leigh turned her anger toward Dawn.

"Yes, it was. He didn't know what he was doing, and I could have stopped it, but chose not to." Dawn now sounded remorseful. "I didn't want him to for selfish reasons, of course. And maybe even a little jealousy on my part." Too many people were getting hurt due to her mistake. It was better when the only feelings involved were hers and hers alone. She didn't even like Leigh, but she knew how it felt to be let down or lied to. The feeling was all too familiar, and she didn't like it at all.

"I know you don't think much of me," Leigh said. "You've thrown insult after insult at me and still I have yet to defend myself. I'm not as dumb as you think I am." She tried hard to blink back the tears forming in her eyes. When she spoke again, her voice cracked giving her exact feelings away. "The worst part about all this is finding out Raheem allowed this to happen."

Raheem opened his mouth to say something, but she held up her hand, cutting him off before a sound had escaped his lips. "Being drunk is not an excuse. I've been drunk many times and I always own up to all my actions."

She shook her head, trying to liberate herself from the thoughts and the emotions she was feeling. It had been a long time since she had felt betrayed by people she held in high esteem. She didn't want to feel or hear anything else. Before the tears could make it down her face, she turned on her heels and headed out the door, slamming it behind her.

This is how I know there is no God, she thought, *because if there was one, why would he continue to inflict pain on me over and over again? What did I do wrong?*

She ran to her car, wanting to put as much space between herself and all the nonsense as quickly as possible.

* * *

Kenyon hadn't spoken a word. He was as shocked as Leigh was regarding Dawn's confession. Ideas and thoughts were going through his mind, and he didn't understand any of it. Something jarred him back to words he had spoken to Dawn, *We all have demons and skeletons hidden. Who are we to judge?* He needed to reassure her that he was a man of his words, stunned, but a promise keeper nonetheless.

"Dawn, I know now and I still want my chance at getting to know you on another level."

Raheem slapped his forehead. "I should have guessed that's why you wanted to know so much. You like her." He laughed. "You've been living with her all this time and you never told her how you feel?"

"I've never told anyone," Kenyon said reprehensibly. "Now you know and what?"

Speaking with his hands, he pointed to the two of them, and shrugged. Currently, it didn't matter to him. The thing on his mind was Leigh; she left hurt and angry. "I did what I intended to do when I invited y'all over and much more than I expected. I hope you both accept my apology, but if you don't that's fine, too." Opening the door to his apartment one last time, he said, "Now you have to get out."

Dawn grabbed her purse and walked through the door, keeping her eyes on the ground. She hadn't looked at either of them in the eyes since Raheem spilled everything. The small ball of dread she was feeling as they were on their way over had now turned into a big pit in her stomach. A sensation of nausea along with the churning in her mid-section made her feel gravely ill. Perspiration was forming on her brow. The drive home in the confines of her car would be pure agony.

All her worrying was for naught. Kenyon opened the door to the car for her, walked around to the driver side, and said nothing about what went on with Raheem. She didn't want to talk about it, so she didn't bother to bring the subject up. She was proud of him though; he hadn't judged her. He was the real deal as far as a good man goes.

As she thought more and more while they made their way home, she wondered what she really found attractive about Raheem. Yes, he was a handsome man and for the most part he had an ok attitude, he could be downright nasty to every and anyone for no real reason.

What does that say about me? she thought. *What am I really looking for in a relationship? Better yet what am I hiding from?*

* * *

Leigh didn't expect to feel such pain in her heart. She couldn't understand why Raheem stayed with her if he wanted Dawn. She recalled him always saying he respected her too much for him to touch her in an intimate way. Other than some intense kissing, he never brushed his hands over any of her body parts that would cause any type of arousals.

She stared at her reflection in the rearview mirror and shook her head. "I was such an idiot. Never again."

She grabbed her cell phone and dialed Rachelle's number. Before Rachelle could say a proper greeting, Leigh said, "I don't want you or Ms. Zinnia calling me and telling me anything about the invisible man you serve."

"Leigh, what in the world are you talking about?" Rachelle asked, baffled.

Leigh noticed she was driving fifteen miles over the speed limit. She took cleansing breaths, but they didn't help at all.

After several moments of silence, Rachelle asked, "Are you there?"

"Don't call me and tell me how good your God is because he hasn't shown me anything good in all my twenty-three years. I know I don't come from a line of wonderful people, but Jesus isn't real. He can't be."

Rachelle tried to use a calmer voice. She didn't want to say anything that for some reason would upset Leigh anymore than she already was. Something clearly had happened since they had lunch the day before.

"Where are you now? Are you on the way to Raheem's?"

"Don't say that liar's name to me," she said loudly.

"Ok," Rachelle said slowly. "I won't. Do you want to come over and talk to me?"

"No I want y'all to go away and leave me alone." Leigh hung up.

Now that she had gotten rid of them, she could go on with living her life like she did before. She stopped at her local liquor package store. She needed something stronger than beer to take away the pain. She purchased a bottle of Grey Goose and Nuvo. The Nuvo she would use to celebrate getting rid of unnecessary emotions and the Grey Goose would be to drown her sorrows in. She had a bottle of tranquilizers the psychologist that she used to see had given her. She's never taken any of them, but tonight she we would take one after the other, one for each person that had hurt her over the years.

When she got back to her place, she hurried inside, opened the bottle of Nuvo, and got her a glass with two ice cubes. She didn't want to try the pink drink for the first time hot. It was in an exotic bottle and it made her happy to have. After pouring the drink into the glass, she took a very long swallow. The carbonation of the drink reminded her of Sprite, but the taste was refreshing.

She drank every drop. She got her Minute Maid Lemonade out the refrigerator to mix with the Grey Goose. By the time midnight came around, Leigh was stumbling all over her apartment. She tried to walk to her bedroom, but was so intoxicated she decided to lie down in the hallway. Her head was spinning too much and she wanted someone to hold the room still.

She spent the night on the floor directly outside the bathroom door.

Chapter Thirty-Four

Sleep eluded Rachelle. She had worried so much about what had happened between Leigh and Raheem. She'd tried calling Raheem most of the night, but all she got was voicemail.

Rachelle had called Ms. Zinnia at six o'clock the next morning, telling her of the conversation she had with Leigh. They were going to meet at the church, head over to Soft Hands where Raheem would be and try to find out where they could locate Leigh. If they were lucky, they'd find out what happened, too, and be supportive in whatever way they could be.

Turning on to the property of the church, Rachelle spotted Ms. Zinnia standing in the front of the building, Bible in hand. No time for formalities, she slowed the car to a roll, allowing her to hop in. She took a left out of the parking lot, headed for the one place they hoped to get answers.

"Welcome, ladies," Kenyon greeted them when the wind chimes above the door clang, announcing their entrance.

Kissing her cousin on the cheek quickly, Rachelle asked, "Where is he?"

His heartbeat sped up. He could see the worry lines in Rachelle's forehead. "He's finishing up with a client. Do I need to interrupt him?"

Nodding, she replied, "Please."

"Ok, I'll be right back."

They watched as he went down the hall, slipped into one of the treatment rooms. He wasn't gone for more than a minute when he returned with Raheem on his heel. He had a towel in his hand, drying off the sage and jasmine massaging oil he had been using.

"What's up? Is something the matter with Dad?" he asked seeing Ms. Zinnia with her.

"No. I need to know where I can find Leigh."

He looked from Ms. Zinnia to Rachelle. *Was she joking?* "You pulled me away from my work to ask me about Leigh?" He went to turn away, but she grabbed his arm, stopping him.

"Tell me where she lives now," she said getting right in his face. "You have been going around treating people like their feelings don't matter for long enough. I don't know what you did to Leigh, but she called me last night sounding strange."

"I didn't do anything." Raheem stood straight as a board. His jaw muscles tightened, teeth gritted, and his hands tightly balled into fists.

Kenyon was standing to the side, witnessing the mess unfolding. He knew why Leigh sounded strange. Dawn and Raheem played a part in that; he had to admit that he also played a part in the whole debacle. Had he not questioned Raheem on what happened, then maybe Raheem wouldn't have felt the need to divulge all the information while apologizing and she wouldn't have over heard all that. They were all to blame. The guilt that was building within him wouldn't allow him to let Raheem walk away pretending nothing happened.

"Yo, man, tell her where she lives before I tell them what's really going on."

"Not you again." He waved them off. "Stay out of this."

"We already know something has taken place between you and Leigh based on what she has told Rachelle," said Zinnia. "While we would love to find out, we'd prefer to know where she lives and that's that. Please tell us."

"She lives off of East Ponce de Leon on Market Street in Clarkson. For the record, she overheard something I was saying to Kenyon and Dawn and that's why she's upset. I didn't do anything to her per se." He rationalized. He said that more for himself than anyone else.

"Please write the address down, so we can get going," said Ms. Zinnia. Along with the slip of paper, Raheem handed over the key Leigh had given him to her apartment.

Rachelle looked at Kenyon before she and Zinnia walked out the spa. She would talk to him later. Right now she needed to get to Leigh. The nagging feeling she had in the pit of her stomach was getting worse. Something wasn't right and she knew it.

Zinnia sat beside Rachelle in the car holding on to her Bible as she prayed. She was speaking so fast that she was making no sense to Rachelle. Ms. Zinnia was the type of person you would want praying for you; she prayed with her whole being. She never once questioned God and the choices he allowed to come into her life. She accepted it all and went along with it.

Rachelle pulled into an apartment complex that looked run down.

"Sweet Jesus," she whispered. There was garbage littering the sidewalk leading up to the dilapidated building. To the left of the door there was a man sleeping under several trash bags. The stairway smelled of urine and kitty litter. "Is this a pre-warning of what we are about to find?"

Urging her to continue on with a supporting hand on her back, Ms. Zinnia reminded her to have faith.

Rachelle knocked on the door, placed her head as close as she could without actually allowing her skin to touch the dirty looking structure. After two minutes of silence passed by, she held her hand out accepting the key that Ms. Zinnia had.

She took a deep breath to blow off the uneasiness she was still feeling. Turning the doorknob, she pushed the barrier open and entered into a space of simplicity. Going from the hallway into Leigh's apartment one wouldn't have guessed there would be such a clean and refreshing space even with the scarcity of the furniture.

Taking slow steps, Rachelle called out, "Leigh, are you here?" Upon closing the door, they saw the hidden hall, where Leigh was sprawled out on the floor. Dropping her purse to the floor, Ms. Zinnia ran over to where she laid.

"Leigh, are you ok?" She shook her trying to wake her. She looked quickly at Rachelle with fear in her eyes. "Dial 911!"

She placed her ear to her chest and she could hear Leigh's heart beating, but her breaths were very shallow. Zinnia went into prayer mode again. She didn't want to feel helpless and at the moment she was experiencing just that. "God, you brought this lost child to us for us to save and we're not going to let you down."

They joined one hand over her body and placed the other on her body. This is the position that they held until the paramedics got there. Rachelle opened the door for them then stayed out of the way as they began to work on Leigh.

"You're taking her to DeKalb Medical Center, correct?" asked Rachelle.

"Yes ma'am," one of them answered as they lifted the stretcher.

They locked Leigh's door and ran to the car. Rachelle yanked out her cell phone, calling Raheem.

She was ticked off with him, but he needed to be there to support Leigh. She needed as many people around her as possible praying for her.

The second phone call she made was to Dawn. She needed to understand what was going on to help Leigh. She was feeling herself back tracking to her protective mode. She hadn't wanted to add another person she feared losing, but here she was scared to death that Leigh wasn't going to make it.

Muttering to herself, Rachelle said, "This is the reason why I didn't want to move forward. I can't deal with this."

"Don't do this to yourself," Ms. Zinnia said. She knew that if Rachelle started feeling skeptical about the new leaf she had turned over, then she would begin recoiling into her shell, placing a barrier between herself and anyone who tried to get close to her. For selfish reasons, she needed to keep Zion's well being in mind. "It was your gut instinct that led us to her. We can only pray we got to her in time."

* * *

Raheem stood in Soft Hands holding his cell in his hand staring at the screen wondering if he had heard Rachelle correctly. The only words registering in his head were Leigh, unconscious, and DeKalb Medical Center. Once he got his legs to cooperate, he ran to the back office, grabbed his keys, and raced out the building. He never bothered to tell Kenyon he was leaving or the news he had just received.

In the car, Raheem did something he had not felt like doing in a long time- he prayed. He prayed harder than he had ever prayed in a long while. It wasn't until he heard the blaring sounds of car horns did he realize he had ran a red light. As luck would have it, a cop was exiting the parking lot on the other side of the street. He turned his lights on and did a u-turn, pulling over Raheem.

Raheem slammed his hand against the steering wheel as he waited for the officer to approach him. "Damn!" he said.

The officer stepped from his black vehicle and made his way to the driver side window. "Do you know why I pulled you over?"

"Yes, officer," said Raheem. "I'm sorry, I didn't mean to do it, but I just got some really bad news."

"Did you want to add more bad news to your already bad news?" asked the officer. "I'm going to need to see your license and registration."

"My girlfriend was found unconscious," he said as he reached into his back pocket for his wallet. "I was only trying to get to her as quickly as possible."

The officer took the cards, but he walked away he said "All the more reason you need to be careful. What good would you be to her if you end up in an accident?"

To Raheem it felt like forever before the officer returned, but it had been only five minutes. The officer handed him back the items with the thin slip of yellow paper, fining him for his stupidity. "Be more careful. And I hope your girlfriend is alright."

Raheem said "Thank you," and waited for the officer to get back in his car before he signaled and pulled away from the curb. He looked at the yellow paper sitting on the passenger seat that signified more than him running a red light. It was a reminder of the number of careless things he had done recently. Most of all the fact he had lost Leigh.

He couldn't stop the tears from rolling down his face.

"If Leigh doesn't pull through, it will be all my fault, and I won't be able to forgive myself," he said aloud before a huge sob escaped his throat.

Chapter Thirty-Five

At the hospital, Rachelle still lamented growing close to Leigh. Her mother's death was enough people going away in her lifetime. She didn't want to see anyone else prettied up in a shiny, over expensive box lowered into the ground. She didn't want to see some random workers throw mounds of soil over the casket.

Her mouth was dry and her heart was pounding. A tightening pain in her chest caused breathing to be difficult. Something wasn't right. Grabbing on to the column in front of the entrance, she bent over, trying to steady her breathing.

"Calm down, honey," Ms. Zinnia said, rubbing her back. "You're having a panic attack."

"I can't breathe," she wheezed. "It hurts so badly."

Zinnia helped her make it to a chair in the waiting area. "Put your head between your legs and take deep slow breaths. Everything will be alright. This is what happens when you take everyone's problems and put them on your shoulders. I know you say you've overcome Lily's death, but you didn't.

Honey, you've put make up and new clothes on top of old wounds."

Rachelle cried out, "It hurts!"

Her words stopped people in their tracks.

A nurse in green scrubs went over to them. "Is she alright?" She took Rachelle's wrist in her hand, looking at the clock on the wall above the elevator, checking her pulse. Next she engaged the stethoscope she had around her neck into her ears and listened to Rachelle's chest.

"Your heart sounds good, but your pulse is racing. Try to stay calm. If I didn't work here, I wouldn't want to be in here visiting a sick loved one either. It's going to be alright."

"Thank you," said Zinnia. As the nurse walked away, Zinnia put her arm around Rachelle and whispered in her ear, "You need to let your mother go."

Tears came from Rachelle without any warning. "I've tried. I can't. All I know how to do is push all my feelings into a space where nobody can see it. And this," she said, looking out into the waiting area, "just makes me remember it all like it happened yesterday."

"I'm going to call Zion to come down here. Right now you need something positive and reassuring to help you calm down. I'm not who you need. Once he gets here, I'm going to check on Leigh." She pulled Rachelle close to her chest. She held on tightly to her and rocked her until she relaxed.

* * *

Zion rushed to the hospital after getting the call from his mother. She had said, "Get to DeKalb Medical quickly. Rachelle needs you." She hadn't told him Rachelle wasn't the patient and he worried that something had happened to her. Going through the sliding doors and seeing them sitting in the lobby, he was able to breathe.

He fell to the ground in front of her and gathered her in his arms. Zinnia left them and went to go check on Raheem and Leigh. She prayed on her way to the emergency room that she would be able to come back to them with good news.

Chapter Thirty-Six

The doctors had pumped out the contents of Leigh's stomach. She was still under suicide watch even though she assured them she hadn't tried to kill herself.

"It was an accident," she protested. "I was angry and wanted the pain to go away."

Her stomach felt so sore, so did her throat. She never wanted to experience this again. Who would intentionally want to go through this?

The nurse had told her Raheem was out in the waiting room asking to see her, but she didn't want to see him. He was the reason she had been in the predicament she was in now. All the years she'd been binge drinking to dull the ache from the pain of being rejected, she had never come close to dying. It took a man to push her far enough to where her life was almost lost. She wondered who found her and how did he know that she was there.

The nurse assigned to keep watch on her came into the cubicle she was in. She checked the straps on her wrist that held her secured to the bed, looked at the IV bag. "There is someone here to see you."

"I told you I don't want to see him."

"It's a woman."

What woman would come to see me? she thought.

"Do you want to see her?" asked the nurse.

Leigh nodded yes. She wanted to know who it was. She had no family or real friends. No one who cared about her just because they wanted they wanted to.

Ms. Zinnia poked her head around the curtain closing Leigh off from the others being treated. Even though Zinnia had a smile on her face, her eyes told a different tale.

"How did you know I was here?"

She stood at the foot of the bed, touched Leigh's covered feet and shook her head at the sight of the straps. "Rachelle and I found you unconscious. We prayed we'd gotten to you in time." She mouthed, *Thank you, Lord.*

Leigh hadn't said anything. She was saying one name over and over again in her head…Rachelle. After the way she spoke to her the night before she didn't believe she would want to have anything else to do with her.

"She told me what you said. What we don't understand is what happened after we had such a good talk the other day? You were opened to talking about what's gone on in your life keeping you from believing and now we have you here, like that. Why?" The smile was officially gone from her face and concern was the only expression visible.

"I felt duped," Leigh replied. "Nothing but the same crap keeps happening to me. People see me and want to take advantage. I have no one, so they figure I have no heart to break. But I do have one…I do." She hadn't cried in a long time and here it was two days in a row she was crying from a broken heart.

"You have Rachelle and me. Why didn't call us to come to you?"

"I don't know. I guess I didn't believe you really cared."

"How long are they going to keep you like that?" she asked, pointing at the restraints. "I would like to counsel you at least three times a week. The agreement we had still stands. I will not try to force God on you. You have to believe in him for yourself."

Leigh wondered if the reason they found her in time had to do with God proving to her he was real.

Chapter Thirty-Seven

Dawn paced the perimeter of the store after she received Rachelle's call. She didn't like hospitals, and she didn't want to face her friend to answer all the questions she would be asking about her involvement with Raheem. She had told her that she knew something took place between the three that clearly upset Leigh enough to where she was now in the hospital.

She didn't want to go and face any accusing eyes. Kenyon hadn't said anything to her on the drive home about what was said and she had been too afraid to even utter a word. She finally understood why her attitude toward Leigh and being judgmental toward her wasn't right. She didn't like being judged either, especially when all the information wasn't known by everyone. "I owe her an apology."

The only thing she could think to do in order to take her mind off everything while she manned the store was to sketch pieces of jewelry she would make later on. At the moment she wished she had some wire and beads with her because she would be bending, beading, and twisting materials into something beautiful to ease the muddled thoughts out of her head.

As she sketched what she called a hope necklace, drawing the center ring that had an opal bead in it, Dawn realized something. She and Leigh were more alike than she would like to admit. Both of their parents had left them willingly and they both were looking for the place where they belonged even if they didn't want to admit it to themselves.

We tend to hate on those most like ourselves, she thought. That's when she called the owner of the store telling her she had an emergency and had to go. She closed up and headed to DeKalb Medical to face the heat she was sure would be waiting for her once she arrived.

The drive over took longer than expected. Dawn questioned what she really wanted and what the proper way to go about getting it was. She never really thought about that before today. She was disappointed in herself for allowing her parents' absence to create such a void that she went from one extreme to the next. She was the shy girl who didn't open up to many and hid from herself. Now she was the person who seduced a man who didn't want seducing, well at least not from her. All along she was looking for was love in places she had no business searching. The only place she should have been looking was in the mirror. If she had loved herself first, then everything else would have fallen into place.

Kenyon and she reached the hospital at the same time. They were approaching each other, staring intently. He wanted so badly to address the way he was feeling, but he couldn't. He wanted her to come to him and speak freely and openly with him, giving him a chance to react in a natural way. After all he was human and he was entitled to his feelings.

"Hey," she said to him.

"You don't like Leigh, so what are you doing here?" he asked.

"I know, but I don't think it's her that I don't like. I think it's how much she reminds me of me that I don't care for." She took the scrunchie off her wrist and pulled her locs into a ponytail. She was nervous and her neck felt as though it were on fire. "You didn't say anything about what happened yesterday. Why?"

"I was waiting on you to come to me." He took off his glasses to clean them and rubbed the bridge of his nose where they had rested.

She cleared her throat and licked her lips. The lump in her throat wouldn't go away no matter how hard she swallowed or cleared her throat. "If you can look past my past, then I can give you a chance. I can't promise you anything, but I am willing to try."

She had taken him off guard. He hadn't expected her to say those words to him. He was trying so hard not to smile. Shocking both of them, he kissed her on the lips. It wasn't anything romantic or sensual, a simple kiss signifying his happiness.

"That's all I've ever asked for."

Hand in hand, they walked into the hospital. They would face Rachelle together. They saw Zion holding her, and they immediately thought the worse had happened.

"Oh no!" cried Dawn. "This is all my fault."

Rachelle and Zion looked up to see them approaching. Rachelle jumped up and ran over to her friend. Pushing her emotions to the side, she pulled her into an embrace. "It will be ok. Leigh will be fine."

Dawn pushed away from her, looking in her face. "You mean she's alive?"

Rachelle nodded.

"So why were you crying?"

"I thought she wasn't going to make it myself. It was scary finding her the way she was. But she's fine."

She breathed a sigh of relief. "I know you want to know what happened, and I will tell you everything, but first I want to go and see her." Rachelle's eyes got big. "Don't worry I'm not going to do or say anything stupid to her."

"You don't owe me an explanation. I'm no one's mother, and I have to realize I can't mother everyone. I need to mother myself and worry about the relationship I'm building with Zion."

* * *

Dawn approached the area where Leigh rested, but stopped when she heard voices behind the curtain.

"Raheem, I can't do this," Leigh said. "I know I'm to blame for introducing you to alcohol, but I can't allow you to bring me down anymore than I already am."

"You can't be serious. I already explained to you what happened. What more do you want from me?" he asked, sounding stressed.

"That's it, nothing. I don't want anything, not even your friendship if that is going to require anything more than I am willing to offer. We're not right for each other. Can't you see that?" she asked in an apologetic way. "We're toxic to each other."

Dawn stood outside the curtain, nodding in agreement. Raheem would have been toxic for her as well. He was all wrong for the type of women she and Leigh were.

"But—" he started to say, but when Dawn entered into the small space, he stopped, looked at both of them, and walked away.

"I guess you're happy to know that Raheem and I are through," Leigh said. "I should never have been with him in the first place."

"Believe it or not, I'm not happy. I heard what you said about him being toxic and those words couldn't be any truer."

She moved closer to Leigh and began undoing the restraints on her wrist. Leigh looked at her, confused. "People like us are too afraid to try to kill ourselves. We run from everything."

"I told them I didn't try to hurt myself, but they wouldn't listen."

"I believe you. I came to tell you that I was wrong about you." She held her hand between hers. "I never gave you a chance.

Leigh showed no emotions. She looked at her knowingly. They had come from different directions, walking the same path.

Chapter Thirty-Eight

Raheem left the hospital grounds without speaking to anyone. He was madder than he'd been in a while. He had a bottle of Jack Daniels waiting for him to get home, and he wouldn't disappoint it.

He didn't want to end up like Leigh, strapped to a bed or having his stomach pumped while people walked around judging him. As he poured the glass of caramel-colored liquid into a glass with a couple pieces of ice, his mother popped into his thoughts. She looked sad in his mind. He knew she wouldn't want this for him.

Raheem did something he didn't think he would ever have to do…he called his father. He needed help.

"Dad, I need you. I need you right now," he said into the phone.

No question asked, Dwight told him he was on his way.

When he got there, Raheem was still staring at the same glass of liquor he had poured for himself when he had first arrived. His mouth had been watering for it, but he didn't want to be sucked into a hole where he couldn't crawl his way out of.

Dwight took the glass and emptied it down the drain. "Are there any others?" he asked as he poured out the remnants of the bottle. Raheem pointed to the cabinets over the stove. He didn't remember when he'd bought all those bottles, but he had.

"I've called Pastor Brown. He's looking for a place that will accept you right away." He looked at his son, long and hard. "We'll get through this together."

"I've tried to be strong for you and Rachelle all these years, Dad. But now Rachelle doesn't need me anymore and when Leigh came along with this salve…" He paused and looked down. He didn't want him to see how weak he really had been all these years. "I placed it over my wound and drowned myself every chance I could so I wouldn't feel useless. Now I don't know how to get away from the hold the bottle has on me."

"You already did the moment you called asking for help."

* * *

Pastor Brown had called Dwight telling him he had found somewhere for Raheem in Florida. They would take him if they could get him there by noon the following day. He packed him a bag with only clothes, his Bible and a framed picture of their family – Raheem, Dwight, Rachelle, and Lily.

When Pastor Brown got there, they were ready to go. Raheem didn't have a chance to call Rachelle to inform her of what was going on, but he'd explain to her later. For now, he knew Zinnia and Zion would look after her until he returned, so he didn't have to worry.

The campus of the rehabilitation center was breathtaking. There was a large lake with a trail that ran alongside it, passing it and going into the woods. The buildings didn't look like it was a treatment center, but more like a spa.

"Son, this is as far as I can get you," Dwight said. "You have to take the last steps by yourself."

Raheem looked over the vastness of the place, placed his hand on the door handle, and the other on the bag with his belongings as a single tear rolled down his cheek.

"I have faith in you and we will see you around Christmas time."

"Thanks, Dad, and you too, Pastor Brown."
Bending down to look inside the car, he said, "Tell
Rachelle I'm sorry I let her down."

Dwight grabbed Raheem's hand and squeezed it.
"Son, you don't know how proud your sister is of you.
You didn't let her down. I'll tell her what you said,
but you know how Rachelle is. She'll be worried about
you. Promise me to take care of yourself and don't
worry about your sister."

"I'm not worried about her anymore. She's
changed a lot."

"Yes, she has. And that's all the more reason
for you to hurry and get better, so you won't miss
her singing for the first time in a long time. She
will want you there."

"I'll try, but I can't and won't promise
anything."

Raheem walked away, disappearing inside the
building.

"Lily, watch over him while he's here," Dwight
prayed.

* * *

A week after he had admitted himself, Raheem
walked the grounds of the facility, mulling over the

things he had heard in group therapy. One lady said writing letters to the people in her life helped her to heal a little more every day. She said, "I even write to those who are no longer living. For all I know they're standing behind me reading over my shoulder while I write. It's odd but comforting just the same."

He had taken a pad and a pen to go find somewhere to sit and be with his thoughts. He had quite a few letters he wanted to write. The first one he wrote had been a long time coming.

Dear Mom,

Where do I begin? When you died part of me went with you. I was so mad at you for leaving us, especially Rachelle. She was your shadow and wanted so much to be like you, but you left her and me to take care of her. I know we had Dad, but he was missing you, too. We couldn't burden him with our emotions.

You missed everything that was important to us. Our senior proms and graduations; those are the things that happened already. We have many more milestones and memorable moments in our futures and you won't be here for those either. Rachelle is going

to get married one day and I will have to stand in
for you again there, too. I can't keep doing it, Mom.
I'm tired.

I stuck the way I felt in my shoes and walked on
it. I had to keep a happy face for Rachelle. You know
she's the baby by two minutes. She never lets me
forget it. We miss you! I wish I knew what I could do
to bring you back. You tell God for me the next time
you sit at his table, I'm mad with him for taking
you. But I understand why he took you. You were
needed there more than you were needed here on earth.
I don't like it because I want to disagree with him.
We needed you because we were your children.

I don't think I can get over this pain if I
don't say I'm sorry to you. Yes, Mom, I'm sorry for
being mad. I hate that you had to go. I will try to
walk the path you would have wanted me to walk.
Love,
Your one and only son
Raheem

He re-read the letter folded it into a paper
airplane, walked into the woods and flew it through
the trees. He couldn't see when it stopped sailing
through the air.

He went back into his room, where he would write the next letter to Rachelle. He didn't get a chance to say goodbye to her before he had left and he hadn't been able to call anyone as yet. They didn't have too many rules in place, but the rules they had were for a reason. Since he had checked himself in, he could check himself out whenever he wanted to. He was told that talking to people on the outside might trigger an urge to get a drink. Already he knew how true that was because every time he thought of Leigh, he wanted a stiff one. She had blew him off to save herself and now he wished he had tried harder with her being who he was and not like the other guys she was used to being with.

He sat at the small desk against the wall, thinking about the words he wanted to write to down. Finally, he began the letter.

Chelle,

Go ahead and be mad because I called you that. Why should we continue to tuck all the things about Mom away? You don't have an answer I bet. That's because we shouldn't. We had many good times, but we forgot about that and lived the past fifteen years on that dreaded Mother's Day. It's time to move on.

Can't say I didn't see this coming. I did. I mean me needing help, not the alcohol. I had gotten help from Pastor and Ms. Zinnia, but no matter how much I got from them, I couldn't give it to you. Once I realized you were doing it without me, well, I felt the first rejection I ever had felt before. That's why I would say the mean stuff that I said to you. I didn't mean them. I hope you always knew this.

You tried to fill Mom's shoes, but you couldn't. I watched you giving it your all during the day, but at night when you fell asleep I could still see the sweet innocence you possessed. But at some point you lost it as we grew up and I became your protector. I have fought every battle there has ever been for you. When you started taking positive steps into the right direction, it almost seemed as though you were leaving me behind. I needed to catch up to you, but I couldn't.

Please don't feel mad. That's not my intentions as I write this letter. All that I want from you is a sister. The kind I can laugh with and fight with, but when all is said and done we are still close.

I hope it isn't too late for you and me.

Love,

Your brother only

Raheem

He wrote several other letters before the day was over. When he laid down that night, his wrist hurt. But he welcomed the pain. He no longer wanted to feel numb. Alive and in pain was way better. At least he knew when he needed a healing if he could feel it.

The sun had been shining even brighter than it had the day before. He opened the blinds allowing the natural light to flood his tiny space. The room wasn't much to look at, but it was enough to live in and think. No televisions or radios were in the rooms. In the community room there was a television and over the public announcement system they played music.

The light from the window landed on the desk, hitting the picture of his family. The beam only highlighted the smiling face of his mother. He took that as a sign.

Chapter Thirty-Nine

It was the day before the Christmas show. To help Rachelle relax, Dawn and Leigh, who after the hospital incident had developed a great relationship, arranged for a beautiful spa day. Only good things allowed, nothing but mud, wax, and hot irons. Dawn wanted to make sure that Rachelle would be able to go see Melody at Hairstyles by Design, so she scheduled an eight o'clock appointment for them at the Serenity Spa.

The ladies met at IHOP for breakfast. Leigh toasted them with a glass of ice cold orange juice. When she first raised her glass, they laughed at her silliness.

"What are you doing?" asked Dawn.

"I'm making a toast." She held her glass even higher. "To the first two real friends I've ever had. I couldn't have asked for a better set of people."

They clang their glasses together and laughed loud enough to attract weird looks, which only triggered more laugher. They were having fun and enjoying life finally. "Let's hurry up and eat so we can get out of here. I can't wait to have my body wrapped in seaweed. I want my skin to feel like a baby's when this day is over," said Rachelle.

Their breakfast was good, but once they wiped their mouth and popped in a couple of breath mints, it was the last thing on their minds. Their day of pampering had finally begun.

"Good morning, ladies," they were greeted by a well made up, bobbed haircut blonde with dazzling blue eyes, wearing pink scrubs and white crocs. "Welcome to the Serenity Spa. I am Pam. I will be your consultant today. Have you decided what you want for your treatment today?"

They shook their heads, their eyes wide at how chipper Pam was. She was so syrupy. "Well, let me recommend some things to you and then we can go from there." She rambled names like hydro mineral wrap, dry skin brushing, and collagen blanket facials. She had their minds reeling.

Leigh said what they all were thinking, "Can you pick some things, and we will do them?"

"Certainly, right this way."

She led them to changing room, found them three empty lockers where they could place their clothes and adorn the white terry cloth robes provided for them. "Take off as much as you want to your own comfort level. I'll be back in five minutes to take you to your first treatment."

Pam took them to a room that smelled of coconuts and vanilla. The lighting was subtle, easy for them to fall asleep while having their massages done. They each climbed onto a table lying face down, preparing for the masseuse. Rachelle and Dawn requested a woman; Leigh didn't care one way or the other. The only stipulation she had was that he had gentle hands and knew what he was doing. Good he was and so were the ladies. When they were done, they felt like their legs were made out of jelly.

"This is the most relaxed I've been in quite some time. Oh my goodness I have been missing out," said Rachelle.

"It only gets better," said Leigh.

"I can't wait," Dawn chimed in.

Pam with her bright smile was back to lead them to yet another room. In this room, the smell of jasmine enveloped them. "Ladies, now it's time for your facials. Once those are done, we will wrap you in seaweed with our secret blend emollient that will detoxify your body while softening your skin and calming your mind."

They took a shower once all their body pampering was completed. Once back in their clothes, they got their nails and toes done. That was the end of their package and it was time for them to get Leigh and Rachelle over to Hairstyles by Design.

* * *

Dawn touched the top of Leigh's curly hair. "With these curls, I guess all you need is a wash and trim. What's that like five minutes in the chair?"

"Be quiet," she said, swatting her hand away. "I keep it short because it's easy. I get up, wet it, add mousse or gel to it and out the door I go. No combs necessary."

"I understand. I haven't used a comb in quite a few years," Dawn said. "I have my locs tightened up and then I style them how I want and that is all there is. Some days I take off my satin cap and go, letting my locs hang, swinging with every step I take." To add dramatization to her words, she shook her head from side to side.

Rachelle had been basking in the day she was having. *This was the way life should have always been*, she thought. Her cell phone rang.

"Hello." She listened. "Ok, I won't. Headed to Hairstyles by Design in the mall to get my hair done." She listened some more. "I'll see you later."

She ended the call, placed her phone back in her purse, and gave no indication of who she spoke to. She just looked ahead, watching the street signs go by.

Rachelle walked slowly from the car to the salon. Leigh and Dawn had to slow down in order for her to keep up with them. When they had come to a complete stop, Dawn placed her hand on her hip and asked, "You that relaxed that you're walking like an old woman?"

"Nope. I'm taking in the brisk air."

She rolled her eyes at her.

Once in front of the shop, Rachelle looked around as though she was looking for someone. Dawn and Leigh joined in to see if they could see who she was looking for. No one looked familiar.

Melody came from the back of the salon, giving out air kisses to Rachelle and Dawn. She looked at

Leigh, then back at the other two. "Is she the one
you told me about?"

"Yes," said Dawn.

"Do you mind?" Melody asked Leigh with her hand
hovering not even an inch away from her head.

Leigh leaned her head closer to her and allowed
her to run her fingers through her tresses.

"Your hair is nice and soft. You don't even need
a trim. It's pretty. I would recommend you touching
up the roots with the color, but other than that I
wouldn't change a thing about your hair."

"Well, thank you." She felt great from the
compliment.

Rachelle walked over to Dawn and placed her
hands on her shoulder, keeping her facing forward.
"Maybe I should change my hair color," she said.

"No!" Melody said. "You're hair is fine the way
it is. I don't want you playing with things you have
no clue about."

"That's why I have you."

Someone cleared their throat behind them. Dawn
turned around. Her eyes got big. There standing
before her was what she thought to be an apparition.

The only reason she knew it wasn't a figment of her mind was because Kenyon was there as well.

"Mom, is that you?"

"Yes, sweetheart, it is." Tears were pooling in the older woman's eyes. Dawn's tears ran right out of her eyes. She felt light headed and her knees began to buckle under her weight.

Kenyon grabbed her before her body could fall. He walked her over to a chair and eased her into it. Melody got a cup of water from the water cooler and Rachelle took a magazine from the counter, fanning her friend with it.

Paula Scott was a lighter shade than Dawn with a few wrinkles and a sprinkling of gray hairs around her hairline. She was shorter with an afro, but otherwise they were mirror images of each other.

"Are you ok?" Rachelle asked her, kneeling in front of her.

She took the water Melody offered and took a few small sips. She looked at her mother again, blinking her eyes quickly trying to make the person in front of her go away. No matter what she did, her mother's face would not disappear.

"Mom, what are you doing here?"

"Kenyon searched for me and asked me to give you the best Christmas present I could ever give you. He said the gift I would receive in return would be to know that you're happy." She took the place of Rachelle kneeling in front of her. "Honey, it's been so long."

Dawn was looking at Kenyon, waiting for him to say something to confirm what her mother had said. Her eyes begged him to tell her anything to make the reality of this day completely real.

"Remember at the dinner party we had at the apartment, we had that discussion about our families?" he asked.

She nodded, as did Rachelle and Leigh. "Well, I saw something in your eyes, a longing for your parents. I made it my mission to find them for you. Your mother is my gift to you for Christmas."

"You did this before—"

"I sure did. And I would have done it after as well. Nothing is better than making the people I love and care about happy."

"Thank you." She hugged him.

She wanted to ask her mother why and how come, but Kenyon had gone through so much trouble to get her here. She wanted to be so mad with her right now, but she couldn't do it. Looking at Rachelle with tears running down her face, who would have loved to be reunited with her mother and Leigh who was smiling brightly at the happy ending, she couldn't take for granted her blessing.

Paula touched Dawn's hair. Her hands moved to her face, her touch so delicate and gentle. "Baby, I'm sorry."

Dawn placed her fingers on her mother's lips, quieting her apology. It didn't matter now. "All that matters is that you're here with me."

They women held on to each other in the entryway of the salon.

"I hate to pull you away from this happy occasion, ladies," Melody said, wiping her tears, "but Rachelle and Leigh, I need to get you ladies going or else we will be here until closing."

"You go spend some time with your mother, and I'll call Zion or my Dad to come pick us up," Rachelle said to Dawn.

She waved goodbye to them and walked off with Kenyon and her mother. Dawn kept her hand over her heart, making sure she was still alive. She looked from side to side. She had Kenyon, the man who loved her for her on one side, and her mother on the other.

"Thank you God for granting me a Christmas miracle," she whispered as a single tear ran down her left cheek.

* * *

Zion had picked up Leigh and Rachelle returning them to their cars.

Before Leigh could get situated in her car, Zion asked, "Are you coming tomorrow?" He held onto her door, awaiting an answer.

Leigh looked at the key in her hand. She couldn't deny that Rachelle was an inspiration to her. But Leigh wasn't sure if church was a place she was ready to go.

"Coming where?" she played dumb. She knew where, but Ms. Zinnia and Rachelle had respected her wishes and did not try to force religion on her. They didn't meet at the church for their therapy sessions. She appreciated the fact that they were women of their words.

Zion sighed. "Look all I'm asking is that you come and support her tomorrow. She's going to need all the friends she has to be there for her. This is a hard task for her. Think about it."

"I know she'll be fine. She's stronger than anyone I've ever known."

"I never said she wouldn't be fine. What I am saying is she would want you there as much as she wants me there." Zion softened his voice "Please come."

"I will think about it, but I won't promise anything."

Chapter Forty

For the past two and a half months, Rachelle had been preparing herself for this very day. She believed that she was ready, but for some reason her nerves were getting the best of her, and she hadn't pulled on her beautiful, red velvet floor length gown. She touched the dress gently; it felt and looked like what love would be visually if it had a body.

"Mommy, I wished you were here to see me today. I want to make you proud," she said, touching the locket around her neck. It was the locket that her father had given her mother fifteen years ago for Mother's Day. The inscription read: *forever my love*. He had been waiting for years to give it to her. Along with the gardenia and ladybug brooch, the locket was the final addition to her elegant attire. Holding the brooch in her hand, she rubbed her fingers over the wings of the ladybug. At one point, the two spots on those wings served as a reminder of all she had left in the world, her father and her brother. Originally, when they had bought the brooch, they had stood for the two kids that Lily had, but now they served as her past and whatever life had to offer her. It was the symbol of her new beginnings.

The night before when her father had given her the locket and the brooch he told her, "These are so you can feel your mother even more than you already do. She would have wanted you to have them and when you have your own children you can give it to them, so they too will have a piece of the grandmother they won't ever have a chance to know."

She had cried, not because she was sad, but because she was proud of how far she had come. But right now she wanted to cry out loud for her mother; instead she would sing from her heart like her father had requested. Rachelle had asked for everyone's input on what song to sing, but they told her they had faith in whatever she picked. Some help they were.

Rachelle sprayed her *Amarge* perfume on her wrist and her collarbone. Slowly she unzipped the dress, taking it off the hanger, and putting it on. She needed to hurry before her father came looking for her.

Standing in front of the mirror, she gave herself a once over. Melody had done an exquisite job on her hair. She had swept it up into an up do that elongated her neck. She looked beautiful and she was ready, butterflies in her stomach and all.

As she descended the staircase, Zion and her father were waiting for her at the bottom. Dwight was holding the camera in his hand, ready to take her picture if she would stop walking long enough for him to focus on her, capturing this moment. He was happy that he could see how happy his daughter...his baby really was finally happy. She was no longer that bitter fifteen year-old that she had been, so angry for all that had happened. Now she was all grown up in every way that counted.

Zion pulled from behind his back a bouquet of red and white roses. He helped her down the rest of the steps. "You look beautiful."

Rachelle blushed. "Thank you. I didn't expect to see you here. We agreed to meet at the church."

"I needed to see you before you got to the church."

She looked confused. Her eyes spoke the words she was afraid to say.

Zion handed the roses to Mr. D., he took Rachelle's hands in his again. "On Thanksgiving, I spoke with Mr. D. and you have been driving me crazy trying to figure out what he said."

She chuckled. "I know."

"Well, he gave me his blessing to ask for your hand and Rachelle, I couldn't let you go into that church today to sing again being the same as you were yesterday." Zion got down on one knee, taking out the ring Ms. Zinnia and he had bought the day after his talk with Mr. D. "You thought I was blowing you off. I wasn't. I only wanted to surprise you with this today. I love you, Rachelle. And nothing would make me happier than you accepting this ring as my promise to you to take care of you and love you from now until Jesus calls us home. Will you marry me?"

She looked from Zion to Dwight and back again. *Could this really be happening*, she thought. *True happiness? Finally?* The warm feeling of the tears she had been holding in all morning rolled down her cheeks, indicating that it was all real.

Rachelle laughed, batting her eyes fast trying to get the tears to stop. Zion was still down on one knee and her father was still there holding the camera and roses, waiting for her to answer. She smiled so big her cheeks began to hurt.

"Are you going to answer the man, or make him stay down there all day waiting?" asked Dwight.

Nodding slowly at first then fast, Rachelle blurted out, "Yes…yes I will."

Zion slipped the ring onto Rachelle's ring finger. The two-carat emerald cut ring looked even better on her hand than it did in the box. They sealed their promise to commit to each other with a warm kiss.

* * *

Rachelle was surprised to see Leigh had made it to church. She had been promising to come, and never did. This day kept getting better and better.

"You made it?"

"I wanted to be there for you like you've been there for me." Leigh genuinely looked happy and excited.

"You look great," said Dwight. "We're glad you could make it. You can have a seat right next to me." He offered her his elbow and the four of them made their way into the sanctuary. Dawn and Kenyon were already there, holding their seats. Dawn especially looked extra elated with her mom on one side of her and Kenyon on the other.

Rachelle looked around and she didn't see Raheem. She was a little disappointed that he didn't make the effort to come and support her. However, he had changed and she now realized that she couldn't save him no matter how hard she tried. They had been trying to save one another all along and forgot about saving themselves. Maybe if they had focused on themselves and had been each other's support system things would have been different. Nevertheless, he was getting the help from the people who could help him, and for that she was grateful. She would continue to support him anyway she could. Currently, praying was all she could and would do for him, hoping he would find his way, as Leigh did. She had come a long way from that lost girl who needed drugs, alcohol, and sex to make her feel as though she was alive.

The program began with the children doing a pantomime skit to the Little Drummer. Rachelle had asked to go last, in case she needed the extra time to calm her nerves. Now she was wishing she had gone whenever they wanted her to because she was calm and happy. She was right where she needed to be at the right time.

"It gives me great pleasure to welcome to the stage a woman who is the daughter I never had. She has a voice like the angels and everyone should have a chance to hear to her sang." The congregation laughed at Ms. Zinnia's attempt of using slang. Placing her hand akimbo, she said, "Yes, I said sang, because what she can do with her voice isn't just singing. Rachelle, come on up here and do your thing."

Rachelle was pulled back from her private thoughts when she heard her name called. She turned to Zion and kissed him lightly before standing. Dwight hugged her tightly, whispering in her ear, "Your mother is proud of you, baby. And we both love you."

She nodded her head and smiled. She didn't feel the need to cry this time. She knew he was telling the truth and that's all that mattered. When she took the microphone from Ms. Zinnia, the ring on her hand caught the light and sparkled. They exchanged a look of knowing and Zinnia smiled, exiting the stage, but not before, she gave her a quick embrace. Except for Dwight, no one knew or even realized that she was wearing the engagement ring until she was on the

stage. She glanced out into the audience and Kenyon
and Dawn was giving her thumbs up.

Rachelle had asked the band to accompany her
with her performance; aside from *What Child is This,*
she also planned to sing a Richard Smallwood song
that would explain how she felt now that she had
crossed over to her new beginnings, "Total Praise."

She sung the Christmas song all the while
looking for Raheem, but he was nowhere that her eyes
could see. He was her twin and it was only right that
she felt as though a part of her was missing. She
felt a pulling at her heart, but she would not give
in to the sadness that wanted to take the place of
her happiness.

As the thunderous applause settled, Rachelle
said, "If you don't mind, ladies and gentlemen, I
have another song on my heart. Do you mind if I sing
it?" Along with her family and friends, the other
members of the church were standing offering
encouragement.

She nodded to the pianist to start. When they
heard the first few chords of the song, amen and
hallelujah could be heard mixed in the melody.
Looking down with her eyes closed, Rachelle took a

deep breath and raised her head as she sang, "Lord, I lift my eyes…," opening her eyes a little more with every word. She saw Raheem standing in the far left on the church.

He blew her a kiss and smiled.

He came, she thought as she sang with every ounce of strength she possessed. She felt her mother's presence surrounding her, and the love, the joy, the happiness Rachelle found sent chills up and through her body as she gave God the praise. *I'm finally alive again.*

Reading Group Guide

1. After her mother's death, Rachelle stopped singing solos. Why do you think she stopped?

2. Why do you believe that Dawn, Rachelle, and Kenyon all kept their feelings, about the person they loved, a secret?

3. Why do you believe the author used two flower names (Zinnia and Lily) for the two mother figures?

4. Everyone handles grief differently. Should Dwight have sought professional help for Rachelle when Lily first died? Why?

5. Raheem and Leigh's relationship was different than the other couples. What were they really looking for from each other?

6. It's said that twins can sometimes feel what the other is feeling. If this is true do you think that Raheem's attitude/behavior changes have something to do with Rachelle's emotional and physical changes? If, yes, why?

7. In society, we tend to prejudge people on first impressions/ glances. Dawn did not like Leigh even before she got a chance to know her. What could have been her issue with Leigh?

8. What do you think was the reason behind Dawn keeping her locs and her talent for making jewelry hidden from her friends?

9. Which character did you like the most? Why? Did you have pity on any of them?

10. If you could choose another ending, what would you write? Why?